One Printers Way
Altona, MB R0G 0B0
Canada

www.friesenpress.com

Copyright © 2024 by N.K. Padua
First Edition — 2024

All rights reserved.

This is a purely work of fiction. While there is an element of historical fiction added to the story, actual historical figures and places had been named to help with the context and I do not claim to own those. The Japanese proverb and a named popular Japanese children's story are also elements I disclaim as mine. They were used to bring the scenes and memories some richness and depth to them. Any name that would probably be the same as with that of an actual person, deceased or alive, are purely coincidental and are a product of my imagination.

No part of this publication may be reproduced in any form, or by any means, electronic or mechanical, including photocopying, recording, or any information browsing, storage, or retrieval system, without permission in writing from FriesenPress.

SBN
78-1-03-831626-4 (Hardcover)
78-1-03-831625-7 (Paperback)
8-1-03-831627-1 (eBook)

ICTION, CULTURAL HERITAGE

tributed to the trade by The Ingram Book Company

DEDICATION

To Mike-ji-san, thank you for your unwavering support;

To Mei-san, thank you for the stories and the shared love for food;

To Ryoko-san, thank you for your passion to share and explain the Japanese culture and history;

To the land and people whose blood I share, even if just a little, whose history, culture, and heritage also shaped who I am now.

1 CORINTHIANS 10:31

AUTHOR'S NOTE

Dear Reader,

Thank you for joining me on this journey, seeing how the story unfolds while also exploring parts of Japanese culture. While I did try to be faithful and accurate towards Japanese traditions, practices, and history, please keep in mind that this story is purely fictional.

To be honest, I struggled with how to convey the story in a faithful way. I struggled with finding the balance of using Japanese words or simply using the English equivalent. I suppose you can say I feared that I might not do Japanese culture justice or that something might get lost in translation. But I have faith in you, Reader, that you'll enjoy the story as much as I did while I endeavoured to stay true to the foundation of communication—making sure the language is clear for the person reading so they can understand my message.

There are some terms I've left in Japanese. That is why there is a glossary you can explore to check for meanings. As an added bonus, I decided to include the names of the characters written in their appropriate Japanese form. You'll find that at the end of the book. It might help in the overall understanding of the story.

Sincerely,

N.K. Padua

GLOSSARY

WAGASHI: Traditional Japanese sweets.

KOHAKUKAN: A term used in the Kansai area; a type of sweet that is usually made during the summer months.

AMAI OMOIDE: Name of the fictional wagashi shop in the story that means "Sweet Memories."

GOSHUGI-BUKURO: A special envelope for goshugi.

GOSHUGI: A monetary gift for weddings.

OBON SEASON: The time of year where the Japanese usually return to their hometowns to visit and offer respect to deceased relatives.

KOTATSU: A low wooden table covered by a futon or a thick blanket with a heat source underneath.

一期一会 **(ICHIGOICHIE – ONCE IN A LIFETIME ENCOUNTER):** A proverb that reminds people to cherish each moment because it will never be repeated; that our encounters with people in this life are only temporary so it is important to treat everyone with respect and to cherish the moments shared with them.

ITADAKIMASU: A phrase roughly translated into "Thank you for the food." Said before starting to eat.

GOCHISOUSAMADESHITA: A phrase also roughly translated into "Thank you for the food," said after eating, especially expressing thanks to the chef.

MESHIAGARE: The Japanese version of "bon appétit" or "dig in."

RONIN: A masterless samurai.

HANAMI: Flower viewing/ cherry blossom viewing; the tradition of enjoying the transient beauty of the cherry blossoms in spring.

SAKURA MOCHI: A light pink rice cake filled with red bean paste and wrapped in a pickled cherry blossom leaf.

NAMAGASHI: Translates to "raw sweets." Traditional Japanese sweets, often synonymous with wagashi. They are made from rice flour and sweet bean paste filling and are delicately shaped by hand to reflect the season. Usually served during a traditional tea ceremony.

SHOGUN: officially *Sei-i Taishōgun* (征夷大将軍 or the Commander-in-Chief of the Expeditionary Force Against the Barbarians). A title held by the military dictator of Japan between 1185 to 1868; nominally appointed by the emperor and considered de facto ruler of the country.

SHISHI (志士)/ISHIN SHISHI (維新志士): A group of political activists during the Edo period who were comprised mostly of ronin who were formerly employed in the Choshu, Tosa, and Higo domains among others. A name usually associated with the anti-shogunate, pro-sonno joi (尊皇攘夷 – "Revere the Emperor, Expel the Barbarian") samurai, but the term is also used by others to address supporters of the shogunate, e.g. the Shinsengumi

SHINSENGUMI: Active from 1863 to 1869; organised by commoners and low-ranking samurai, it was a small and elite group of swordsmen.

SEPPUKU: A form of ritualistic suicide

KURI KINTON: Candied chestnut and sweet potatoes. Prepared as part of the osechi ryori (Japanese New Year's food); symbolises economic fortune and wealth

DAIFUKU: a type of wagashi. A rice cake (mochi) that has a small, circular filling like sweet red bean paste or other ingredients and is dusted lightly with potato starch

TOSHIKOSHI SOBA: known as the "year-crossing soba." Typically eaten on New Year's Eve, the soba noodles are believed to represent longevity. It is often considered bad luck to have uneaten noodles before the beginning of the new year.

KAGAMI MOCHI: Translated as "mirror mochi." A decoration usually seen on walls or in the windows of Japanese homes. It consists of two mochi, a smaller one stacked atop a larger one, and has a daidai (bitter orange) or mikan (Japanese orange) on top. It is usually on display until the first week of January at which time it is then eaten by the family by adding the broken down mochi to New Year's soup known as ozoni. While it does not look a mirror, in Shinto, the circle is believe to represent the mirror of the highest deity, the sun goddess Amaterasu.

HATSUMODE: The first visit to a shrine for the New Year to pray for blessings.

NAGOSHI NO HARAE: A purification ritual of summer's passing that's performed on the last day of June; it allows people to cleanse themselves from misdeeds and negativity that has accumulated during the first six months of the year, and to pray for the next half of the year.

PROLOGUE

Reina stretched her arms above her head, relieved that she had finished studying for the day. It was the last week of July, and Kyoto's Gion festival had just ended. It also meant, for students like her, the summer holidays. She had a lot of homework to do, including getting her thesis done. She loved what she was studying and didn't mind all the hard work.

"Remember to confirm the requirements for graduate school on Monday :)"

She couldn't help but smile as she re-read the reminder she wrote on a sticky note. She had mixed feelings; a part of her was excited that she was about to finish university, but another part of her was anxious about her future. While she loved what she had been studying at university and wanted to further her education related to language and literature, she knew that she would one day take over Amai Omoide. The store had been in the family for generations. The responsibility of preserving the family legacy would eventually fall upon her shoulders.

Shrugging it off as normal, Reina started massaging her muscles while considering what she wanted to cook for dinner. Studying non-stop for the past few hours made her neck and shoulder muscles hate her. Nothing new though.

As she rummaged through her refrigerator, her phone started ringing. Walking back quickly toward her table, she saw the screen flashing her uncle's number. Reina answered without much thought. "Hello?"

"Good afternoon. Is this Reina Maruyama?"

She drew her phone away from her ear in confusion when an unknown voice came through from the other end. She double-checked. It was her uncle's number. "Yes?"

"I am calling from…"

Reina could feel herself freeze the more she listened to the person calling. Blood quickly drained from her face as shock took over.

CHAPTER 1

"Thank you for coming," Reina said as she bowed towards the last customers of the day. It was only noon, but it was decided that they would close shop early. The elderly couple waved one last time before turning around and walking away.

As she watched them go, Reina couldn't help but sigh. They never closed early, but given the circumstances, everybody was too concerned to keep working. The head of the family—also the current head Japanese sweets artisan—was in the hospital fighting for his life. Reina herself was working on adrenalin having had no sleep, no appetite, all while making sure she fulfilled her responsibility.

The past twenty-four hours were almost a blur. The phone call changed everything. She felt like an observer of her own life, outside her own body. It didn't feel real, yet she was cognizant of reality. She sighed again, silently hoping that the adrenaline coursing through her veins would last longer because she couldn't afford to crash.

Reina walked back into the shop and turned the shop sign to *closed*. She headed behind the curtain, which bore the shop logo and her family crest, to the small cabinet of well-organised cleaning supplies. Without a thought, she went through her daily routine of cleaning up the place. A force of habit she disciplined herself into.

Her grandparents had left to go to the hospital early, wanting to be there when they transferred her uncle, Ichigo, from the ICU to a regular room. All of them had been at the hospital for hours the night before. They sat in silence in the waiting room while the doctors did their tests and examinations.

Ichigo had immediately been placed in the ICU after life-saving procedures were performed on him at the emergency department. After he was stabilised, doctors wanted to do a more thorough series of tests.

It was hours before a doctor finally met with them. The doctor explained that Ichigo had suffered a stroke. As shocking and horrifying as it was to hear, the doctor was also quick to explain that he had received medical treatment on time, giving him a higher chance of recovery. But they were also cautioned that the next few hours were critical, which was why they wanted to keep him at the ICU overnight for observation. It was also explained to the family that the medical team had induced a coma to allow his body time to recover, but they would slowly bring him out of it in the next few days.

The doctors advised the family to head home because they would not be able to see him while he was in the ICU, and visiting hours were over for the day.

Reina told her grandparents that she was going to take care of the shop. She had been working side by side with her grandparents and uncle since moving back to Kyoto. At that time, her grandfather was still the head of the family and the head artisan. She loved watching her grandfather and uncle make those delicate sweets until they started teaching her how to make them herself.

As the years passed and with her grandfather experienced more pain because of arthritis, Reina started to shoulder more responsibilities in the family business, especially in the kitchen, while her uncle took over the family and the head artisan position. Things settled given their new dynamics.

The stroke had taken everybody by surprise. Ichigo never presented any signs or symptoms that he was not feeling well.

No one could remember hearing him complain about anything health related.

No matter how much her uncle's situation blindsided her, Reina chose to step up and work. The day after still proved to be overwhelming. Kouji knew his granddaughter well. While he was confident that she had the necessary experience to create the delicate confections their store was known for, she would be distracted because of Ichigo. Although Reina was responsible, he couldn't expect her to be unaffected by what'd happened to her uncle. Kouji's eldest son, Ichigo, had taken on being Reina's father figure. They were extremely close.

Reina was going through her mental checklist of things to get done as she wiped the table. She was so focused she almost missed the bell chiming behind her, signalling someone's arrival. The sound brought her out of her musing.

"Good afternoon. I'm sorry, but we are…" she started saying as she turned towards the person who entered. "…closed."

A tall man stood in the entryway, looking at her. Her heart just about stopped. He smiled at her. "Hello, Rei. I'm not sure if you remember me—

"Hajime."

Her automatic response widened his smile. "It's nice to see you again." With that, he opened his arms just like he used to when they were children. And just like when they were kids, Reina flew to him, wrapping her arms around him in a tight embrace. Hajime didn't think twice as he did the same.

Just before Reina could say anything, the curtain was moved out of the way and one of the shop employees, Mio, walked out. "Reina, we—" She stopped short. The other employee, Sayaka, was confused as she bumped into her and looked up to see what was going on.

Sayaka couldn't help but smile. "Hajime! It's nice to see you again."

Reina and Hajime took a step away from each other, sporting slight blushes on their faces. Sayaka bit the inside of her cheek to stop herself from laughing.

"It's nice to see you again too, Mrs. Ito. How have you been?" Hajime answered as he looked at the older woman.

"I'm doing well, thank you. Are you back on vacation or finally staying?"

"Ah! I'm back to stay. I believe my mom has been sharing her thoughts about it. She hasn't been subtle in hinting about her preference." Hajime answered.

"You can't blame her, dear." Sayaka replied as she and Mio walked closer.

"Well, that's true. Your mom has never been subtle about that," said Reina, "it's great to have you back, Hajime. Let me introduce Mio. I'm not sure if you have met her." She gestured towards Mio, then went on, "Mio, this is Hajime Yoshida, Mrs. Yoshida's third son." Turning to Hajime, she continued, "Hajime, this is Mio Fujiwara. We pretty much started working here at the same time."

"It's nice to meet you, Mr. Yoshida." Mio bowed, which Hajime reciprocated.

"Anyway, we have finished cleaning at the back, so we will be heading out. Are you sure you're okay closing on your own?" Sayaka addressed Reina.

The young lady smiled and bowed to thank the older woman for her thoughtfulness. "It's fine, Mrs. Ito."

Sayaka nodded. "Well, see you tomorrow then. Please let me know when it will be okay to visit your uncle." With that, the two ladies walked to the door.

Reina sighed, closing her eyes just as Hajime directed his questioning gaze towards her. "Would you like some tea?" She asked as she took her cleaning supplies back. No one knew about her uncle aside from her family and the staff.

Reina hadn't seen Hajime since she was twelve. His mom always had stories about him and often expressed how she wished he would settle at least in Japan again. Hajime had been away in France since after he graduated from secondary school. Reina was happy to get to see him again, but she pictured the reunion completely differently. She knew Hajime was wondering what was going with the early closure of the shop and the comment from Sayaka.

Without waiting for his reply, she turned on the kettle and started to prepare tea. Hajime had followed her behind the counter, quietly observing her. Although he hadn't seen her in years, he could still see the little girl he once knew. She would tell him what was going on was when she was ready.

"Is there anything I can do to help?" Hajime offered instead.

Reina glanced back at him. "There's an ice box beside you. The serving plates and cutlery are to your left. If you don't mind preparing some of the kohakukan, that would be great. You can choose anything you find there."

When Hajime opened the container, he couldn't help but be impressed with what he saw. The sweet, translucent jelly cubes of the kohakukan were prepared so delicately that they seemed like those glass sculptures people liked to buy as souvenirs. There were different designs—goldfish in the middle of the jelly, making it look like it was swimming, summer flowers like hydrangeas, and more.

The two worked in silence before settling down at one of the tables to talk.

CHAPTER 2

"Rei, don't think I haven't noticed that you are almost dead on your feet. Aside from kohakukan and green tea, have you eaten anything else yet?"

At Hajime's pointed question, Reina blushed and looked away. Hajime sighed. Her answer was loud and clear in her silence. He gently took her hand and started walking, leading the way to his house. "I'm feeding you first. If you are still somewhat awake after, I'm driving you to the hospital."

"But—"

"No *buts*, Rei," Hajime cut off. "I understand you are worried about Mr. Maruyama but that doesn't mean you are going to forget about yourself." He did not need to look back to know what she was thinking, which was likely written all over her face.

Hajime's family lived in a shrine not too far from where Amai Omoide was located. The traditional Japanese sweets store Reina's family had owned and operated for generations had been one of the main landmarks in their part of Kyoto just like his family's shrine.

"You can let go now, Hajime." Reina's soft voice brought Hajime out of his thoughts. Wordlessly, he let go and glanced at her a bit. "Thanks for still looking out for me."

Hajime commented softly, "We might not have seen each other for years, Rei, but that doesn't mean that I stopped caring about you."

Reina blushed. "Thanks again." Hajime ruffled her hair, which made her exclaim "Hey!" automatically as she tried to get away from him. He was successful in making her smile.

"I'm home," Hajime called out as soon as he and Reina walked through the front door. His mom's "Welcome back" immediately followed. Yuuka Yoshida was drying her hands on a small towel as she walked towards them. She was pleasantly surprised to see who accompanied her son. Reina bowed and greeted her.

"Rei! Come in! Come in!" She ushered the young woman inside. "How are you?"

"I'm fine. Thank you, Mrs. Yoshida. I'm sorry for intruding like this, but Hajime wasn't taking no for an answer."

Hajime snorted and said, "I'm feeding you, and I'm not letting you out of my sight until I'm sure that you have eaten enough." He walked over to the kitchen and opened the refrigerator. "Have you eaten, Mom?"

"I was just about to start lunch." Yuuka then turned towards Reina. "You haven't eaten, Rei? You know you're always welcome here."

Reina bowed. "I'm sorry for imposing, Mrs. Yoshida. Thank you for having me."

The older woman smiled warmly and patted the younger woman on her shoulder.

"Oh!" Reina suddenly remembered the box of sweets she packed for the Yoshidas. Hajime had mentioned that he had stopped by Amai Omoide to get some. She'd packed the remaining kohakuhan and presented it to him, but when he realised earlier that she hadn't eaten anything else, he all but frog-marched her out of the store, leaving the box with Reina.

"How are your grandparents and uncle?" Yuuka asked as she received the box.

Reina wavered. Although the Yoshidas were close to her family, she still hesitated in revealing what was happening. A part of her didn't want to acknowledge that what happened to her uncle was real. As irrational as it were, for a split second it seemed that if she didn't say it, she could pretend it weren't true. Reina knew better and plucked her courage to admit, "My uncle is in the hospital." At Yuuka's gasp, Reina was quick to add, "He's stable. My grandparents are there. They sent a message earlier saying that he has been transferred out of the ICU. He's still in a medically induced coma, but Grandmother said he's stable. The doctors are optimistic, she said."

Yuuka engulfed Reina in a warm, motherly hug. "Oh, my dear," she whispered, "Ichigo is a strong man. He will be okay."

All the stress overwhelmed Reina. It had been a long time since she had felt a mother's embrace. She couldn't help it. She buried her face on Yuuka's shoulder as tears started to fall. Yuuka's motherly instinct had gone out towards the younger woman. She tried to comfort her as she would any of her children.

"There, there, Rei," She crooned as she guided Reina towards the sofa. "Let's sit down while Hajime finishes cooking,"

***

Hajime had watched the ladies while he was cooking. Their voices were so soft that it was hardly audible from where he stood. Whatever it was they were talking about, Hajime could guess that after his mother comforted Reina, she chose a completely different topic to divert her attention to something else. It would have been a brief reprieve.

It wasn't long before his mother was able to engage Reina in what looked like an interesting discussion. She definitely looked livelier than she had earlier. Her fatigue was still glaringly obvious though. He watched her struggle through lunch. It was painful for Hajime to watch Reina fight herself to keep awake. When she offered to help out in the cleaning, he finally had enough and told her to go to the living room to wait for him. Yuuka was persistent in not allowing her as well. With a sigh, she did as she was told.

With both mother and son at work, it didn't take long to get things in order. Hajime walked over and noticed that Reina had fallen asleep. He knew the chances of that happening were very high. It was his intention to get her to rest, so he couldn't help feeling proud it worked.

Hajime bent over, picked her up, and carried her to his room. She would have a more restful sleep there.

Apparently, his mother had the same thought. As soon as he came back after settling Reina on his bed, Yuuka was on the phone with Yuzuki. Reina's grandmother was very thankful to hear that they had made sure her granddaughter was fed and resting. The older woman asked Yuuka to tell Reina when she awoke that she wasn't expected until dinner. The two women chatted for a while.

Hajime and his mother had packed several lunch boxes for the elderly couple who were still at the hospital as they waited for Reina to awaken. Having left enough food for his father and brothers, Hajime and his mother accompanied Reina to the hospital once she'd freshened up.

Seeing Ichigo Maruyuma unconscious with all those machines attached to him was a sobering experience. He had always been a person with a big, happy, and sociable personality. It was disconcerting to witness him on that hospital bed. It reassured everyone, though, to know that as the hours passed, the doctors seemed increasingly optimistic. It was only a matter of time before Ichigo would find his feet again.

When visiting hours were over, the elderly Maruyama couple had insisted that Reina head home. Hajime and Yuuka offered to drop her off, which Reina graciously accepted when her grandparents sought out Ichigo's doctor.

Hajime noticed the fatigue on Reina's features. The nap she took earlier hadn't been enough. He wanted to make sure that she made it home safe. Looking out for her was something he always did in their youth. His instincts were pushing him to continue the behaviour from the moment they reconnected earlier. Driving Reina home gave him peace of mind. Ever the gentleman his mother raised him to be, Hajime walked Reina up and ensured she got into her apartment and locked the door.

The drive home from Reina's apartment complex was a quiet one. Hajime found himself reflecting on everything that had happened during the past few hours.

"What do you think about the situation, Hajime?" His mother's quiet question broke him from his thoughts. He gave her a quick glance before looking back towards the road. She then continued, "Kouji's concern is valid. His granddaughter will need help. They need help. Rei is capable and is turning out to be a wonderful artisan herself, but he did make a valid point. At the end of the day, Rei is still a student—a graduating student. If I'm not mistaken, she's currently working on her thesis." Reina's grandfather had intimated with them his concerns regarding his granddaughter.

Hajime didn't answer right away. He slowed the car down at the red light. He looked towards his mother and said, "I've already told Mr. Maruyama that I would help. He offered to hire me. I'll be meeting with Rei's grandfather tomorrow to talk more about it and a possible contract."

CHAPTER 3

It was six in the evening. Hajime and Reina were settled on the tatami mat of the receiving room of her grandparents' house, a pot of green tea was on the low table between them. They had just finished closing the shop. For the past week, they'd both worked closely with Kouji and Yuzuki.

Kouji, even with his arthritis, could still create sweets but not as detailed or as much as before. He had asked Hajime to stop by his house as he showed the younger man some of the more popular ones the store produced during summer. Kouji had confidence that while Hajime was not trained in traditional Japanese sweets craftsmanship, his experience as a professional pâtissier would come in handy. It wasn't a difficult decision to hire Hajime.

That evening was a little different; they decided to go over the books instead. With Ichigo in recovery and his doctors having warned them that it would take a while for him to recover, Kouji and his wife knew they would need more help from their granddaughter and Hajime. The two would have to be more involved with the management of the shop.

Reina still had her school obligations to finish, and Kouji didn't want her to sacrifice her studies months before her graduation.

"The store is afloat but hasn't been doing well these past few months. We have maintained things as best we could but circumstances as they are…well, something needs to change." Kouji took a sip of his tea.

Turning the page of one of the record books, Hajime commented, "With the status of the economy as it is, it's impressive that Amai Omoide has been stable. True, it's not flourishing, but at least it's stable." Closing the book, he then turned to look at the older man. "I was talking about it with my brother and Masashi commented that their company is finally starting to recover. They were in an even worse situation. He said that almost half the workforce had to be let go last year."

"What kind of changes are you thinking, Grandfather?" Reina then asked.

Kouji didn't answer right away. It was a good question.

Amai Omoide had been the Maruyama family's business from the Tokugawa era. Kouji's great, great, great grandfather had moved the family from Shinano province, now known as Nagano prefecture, to Kyoto. The man had thought that Kyoto would serve as a fresh start since it was the imperial capital during the Edo period. While it was a new beginning for him and his family, as well as the birth of Amai Omoide in 1860, the blood and turbulent transition that started in the 1860s threatened the fledgling store. By fate's intervention and advice from unexpected sources, the family was able to survive through to the Meiji era all the way to the contemporary moment. Now, it will need to adapt and change to survive again.

***

1860, First year of Man'en, Edo Period

"How are you feeling, Shiori?" Riku Maruyama asked as he glanced back towards his wife.

They had been travelling on the Nakasendo highway on foot for quite some time. They had left Shinano province and decided to head to Kyoto, the capital. It had been a heart-breaking decision to abandon the only home they both knew. There was no choice. It was leave or die.

The local gangs in their small town got more and more aggressive against one another. After a week of one faction hiring ronin for their conflicts, things boiled over. The once peaceful town was bathed in blood. Their sweets shop was raided. The rest of their extended family were slaughtered just like those caught in different stores and the main road.

Together with some of their neighbours—any person who could— Riku and Shiori took their infant son and ran.

Riku had taken what money they had saved at home—whatever wasn't stolen— grabbed a few personal belongings and led his wife and child son out of town. The small family had fled in a panic, not sure if they would make it out with their lives. The image of people lying underneath pools of blood, being slaughtered without mercy, and the screams that eventually faded into an eerie silence became constant companions to their exhausted and terrified minds. They plagued Riku and Shiori's thoughts constantly, regardless of whether they were awake or asleep.

There had been no time to give their loved ones a proper burial, making it an even more painful experience. The guilt of not being able to send off family and friends in death was immense, but the young parents pushed to survive.

From atop a hill, they watched their small town burn into the night. It had been difficult to grieve, especially with a young son barely a month old. It was the middle of March, and the weather was still frigid. How to survive and keep their infant alive took precedence above anything else.

Riku worried about his family. He could only hope that all of them would survive the trip to Kyoto. Disregarding any fatigue he felt, Riku urged and encouraged his wife to continue walking. The faster they could reach Kyoto, the greater the chances they'd survive.

Shiori stopped walking beside her husband. She carefully pushed back the blanket they used to keep their son as warm as possible. "Kouki is thankfully doing okay. I'm also all right, Riku. Are you okay?"

He smiled to reassure his wife. "We arrived in Kyoto just in time. There's enough daylight left that we can find an inn for the night. I *want the two of you in a warm bed tonight."* He could see the relief on Shiori's face.

Asking the locals, they were able to secure a room and their first warm meal for the day.

Once they'd settled in for sleep, Shiori couldn't help but ask, "What are we going to do now, Riku?"

Her husband gave a heavy sigh. "It would be hard, but the only thing we can do is to start another store here. It will be next to impossible, especially with all the competition in the capital, but we can only do our best."

Shiori was silent for a moment before she nodded. "Are we naming the store the same?"

Riku shook his head. "While Omoide has been the Maruyama brand for generations, this is our new start. I was thinking…how about Amai Omoide?"

***

"We are a small family business, but we have always managed to adjust with the times," Kouji started. "We will do so again." Looking at his granddaughter, he said, "Tradditional Japanese sweets are something everyone in our country learns to appreciate throughout their lives. We eat them for special occasions and the like. It perfectly complements green tea. It's important to preserve our culture but at the same time find a new way of sharing it."

"That is an important thing to consider," Hajime said.

Reina reflected on what her grandfather had said. He hadn't shared any kind of plan, but what his words warranted consideration going forward.

"Are you thinking of anything in particular, Mr. Maruyama?" Hajime went on to ask.

"Before I answer that, let me ask your thoughts about this. You as well Rei."

Hajime and Reina glanced at each other. Reina encouraged Hajime to answer first.

"Kyoto is one of the cities in Japan where we celebrate our history and culture. Speaking about business, though, we need a plan that honours Amai Omoide's history. If we are going to make changes or introduce something new, it shouldn't contradict what the shop has stood for. At the same time, the idea should be fresh enough to generate more business."

The older man nodded. He then turned towards his granddaughter, prompting her to speak.

Reina carefully thought out her answer. "Sweets from Amai Omoide, watching you, Uncle Ichigo, and Dad in the kitchen… those are my sweet memories. Those were the things I remembered while living with Mom and Mr. Suzuki in Tokyo. I often watched customers as a little girl and saw them smiling when they left the store. Some couldn't hide their eagerness and excitement looking at the different sweets. I'd like for that to continue. I want more customers to have a little bit of happiness from us, their own amai omoide, their own precious, sweet memories. I agree with Hajime as well."

Kouji smiled fondly at his granddaughter. He knew she didn't have an easy time when she was in Tokyo. He nodded before saying, "As of now, we sell traditional sweets and tea. Most take them are taken home, but we have a few tables for those who would like to eat at the shop. What if we observe afternoon tea?"

"Afternoon tea? I'm not sure I understand." Reina commented while Hajime silently agreed with her.

"We already sell tea and wagashi. Why not allow our customers to enjoy a complete afternoon tea experience?" Kouji patiently explained.

Hajime contemplated what the old man was saying. "Please correct me if I'm wrong, Mr. Maruyama, but are you suggesting we offer afternoon tea like cafes?"

Kouji nodded. "That's exactly what I was thinking."

"I understand now what you are saying, Grandfather, but I think we should also think about the layout of the shop. If I were the customer, the ambiance would also be something I'd consider. It's an important part of the experience."

Kouji opened the record books again to show Reina and Hajime. "As we have discussed, we are doing okay. We can afford to close the front part of the store and renovate it. We can set up display cases in front of the store and continue to sell sweets. It won't be as much, but it will still generate income while we renovate. I will have to verify it with city hall first, though. Regardless, even if we aren't allowed, there is enough savings to prevent the shop from going bankrupt for at least six months."

"Pardon me for saying this," Hajime politely commented, "but I think a complete closure would be more appropriate. Given the current structure, a curtain is the only thing that separates the front of the store from the kitchen. If there is construction being done in the front, it will more than likely violate safety and hygiene protocols for kitchens. Also, since a new service will be offered, it will be good to take the time to familiarise ourselves with how we want to offer it. Mrs. Ito and Mio would also need to undergo new training."

Reina knew that Hajime had experience working in pastry shops and restaurants in Paris. With the highly competitive market they had there, she trusted his point of view. She glanced towards her grandfather, who seemed to trust Hajime's comments too.

Kouji just smiled. He got up and walked towards a bookshelf nearby. Hajime and Reina exchanged glances. They watched as the older gentleman took out what looked like another notebook—an older one. They waited as he walked back and sat down. Running a hand lovingly on top of the cover, his eyes reflected a bit of sorrow and nostalgia. "It seems that a complete halt of business is a better option while we renovate and get all the staff acquainted with the afternoon tea plan. Perhaps this is also the time to put into action this particular plan." He then handed the notebook to Reina.

It confused her at first, but when she looked at the cover, a shocked breath left her. She recognised the handwriting very well. She couldn't help the tears that pricked her eyes. "Dad?" she breathlessly asked her grandfather.

He smiled. "Your father, Yuuki, was a brilliant businessman. He had started that just before he began feeling ill. He had left instructions and documents with your uncle before he passed. That notebook was one of them. After he passed, your uncle and I decided to keep it on hold."

As Reina started reading through her father's notes, Hajime looked over her shoulder to see. Both of them were in awe. The details were already impressive, but the phases of the plan got them more and more excited as they read along.

CHAPTER 4

After dinner, Hajime walked Reina home. They decided that they'd implement Yuuki's plan. As surprising as it was, the entire vision fit what they were hoping to achieve.

"I vaguely remember dad always writing in a notebook. I always thought it was his journal. He left a lot of notebooks with my uncle before he died. Uncle Ichigo gave me all of them when I came to live back here in Kyoto...well, what I thought was all of them. I didn't know there was another one grandfather was keeping."

Hajime looked at Reina. "I remember your dad. He was a nice man. I remember he loved to laugh just like your uncle."

That made Reina smile. That was one thing she missed about her dad. He always knew how to laugh made her smile whenever she felt sad. "I miss him."

A newfound silence enveloped them as her comment drifted off in the wind.

"Did he give hints about the restructuring plans written in the ones you have?" He asked quietly after a while.

"No. The most of his journals were mixed with his memories, his realisations, what made him laugh, his concerns, those kinds of things. The specific journal was..." Reina trailed off and took a deep breath before continuing. "He addressed each entry to me. Confessions, pieces of wisdom, advice for certain situations, wishes and hopes for my life that he said he'd anticipate from heaven...that no matter what, he will make sure I feel his love from heaven."

Hajime reached out and squeezed her hand. "He was more than brilliant businessman. He was also an amazing father." She squeezed his hand in thanks, and after a beat, he went on, "You said that it was only when you returned to Kyoto that your uncle gave you your father's diaries?"

Reina released a sigh. "Yes. It was under dad's instruction. He knew he was dying. He made the appropriate preparations. One day, when I was in school and mom was out, he had Uncle Ichigo come over. Uncle Ichigo said that Dad explained how he loved mom but knew that once he was gone, she would more than likely throw his things away. She wouldn't be able to keep sentimental things—it would be too painful for her. To make sure that I got the diaries and other personal things dad wanted me to have, he gave them all to Uncle Ichigo."

Hajime could vaguely remember that time. He was twelve when Reina's father's health started declining. He was thirteen when her father passed. It took another year before Reina's mother took her and relocated them to Tokyo. He had only seen Reina few times after that, always during long vacations, but that stopped when he was seventeen. She'd stopped coming to Kyoto all together.

When he'd left for France to study, his mother had informed him that Reina had returned to Kyoto for good. He never asked his mom what happened nor did Yuuka offer much information about it. If he thought back, he rarely heard anything about Reina's mother, Reika. The only thing he remembered was that she was sweet.

"Does your mom know that you have your dad's journals?"

Reina shook her head. "After I moved to Kyoto, we lost contact. It's not that I don't try, but she never replies." She sighed. "I can't say that it really surprises me because she started pulling away the moment dad got sick. When we moved to Tokyo, she had to work. She came home late often. When she started dating Mr. Suzuki, it was like her whole world revolved around him, and I was an afterthought."

"I'm sorry."

"No, please. No need to apologise. I've accepted that mom is who she is. It doesn't make me love her less."

"And Mr. Suzuki?"

Reina hesitated. Her relationship with her stepfather wasn't amicable. She tolerated him because of her mother. He did pay for her education while she lived with them but they didn't really have a bond. "He's all right, I suppose. I think our relationship is better now that we don't spend time together." She shook her head and smiled, hoping to dispel the negativity around them. "Enough about me. I never asked you, but what's it like in France? What was it like studying there? Training? Working?"

Before Hajime could answer, a male voice called out, "Reina? Is that you?" Both of them stopped and looked to their left as a man walked towards them.

When Reina realised who it was, she said, "Ah! Satoshi! Good evening." There was a subtle change in her tone. The cooler tone to her voice made Hajime glance at her. When Reina turned to Hajime, she was surprised to see that he was already looking at her. Without missing a beat, she added, "Hajime, this is Satoshi Fujii, my upperclassman at university."

"Good evening. I'm Hajime Yoshida. Nice to meet you." He gave a bow towards Reina's schoolmate. Hajime looked to the other man and tempered his facial expression. He kept a polite facade. There was no indication that Satoshi noticed the drop in Reina's voice. Either the man was deliberately being obtuse or honestly didn't notice.

"Nice to meet you too, Hajime." Satoshi reciprocated the bow. There was a standoffish look in his eyes. "How is your summer vacation? It's about time to be doing your thesis." He addressed Reina, focusing all his attention on her.

Reina took a moment to take a breath. She silently hoped she was successful in keeping her discomfort from her face. "It's okay. My thesis is progressing well, I think. I was working with my advisor yesterday. She's satisfied with my progress so far." She respected Satoshi's intellectual prowess. He was simply brilliant. She and her classmates had, at one point or another, benefited from his sound advice and academic support. Lately, Reina started feeling uncomfortable towards Satoshi's attention and advances.

"That's good," Satoshi commented. "Well, if you need any help, let me know. You're still planning to apply to graduate school, right?"

Reina nodded and offered a small bow. "Thank you." No matter how frustrated she was with Satoshi, he was still her upperclassman in school. It was an ingrained habit to be polite. There was no good excuse to be impolite to someone.

Satoshi bowed back. "Have a good evening."

"You too."

"Again, it was nice to meet you, Hajime. Have a good evening." With that, Satoshi left Hajime and Reina alone.

Hajime raised an eyebrow at Reina.

"What?" She blinked at him.

"Nothing." He smirked as he began walking. "Boyfriend?"

"No, of course not!"

"Such strong denial," Hajime teased.

Reina resisted the urge to roll her eyes. "Whatever, Hajime."

After a beat, Hajime asked, "Does he know?"

Reina tilted her head and frowned. "Know what?"

"That you don't think of him romantically."

Reina sighed. It was a tired sigh. "I respect him as my upperclassman. I'll admit. He's not exactly someone I hang out with. As a research partner? I don't mind. But...his current behaviour towards me is not something I comfortable with. He does go out of his way for me sometimes, too much lately if you ask me. To be fair though, it's always related to academics. He's never outright approached me romantically. But...I don't think I'm being conceited to say that I do notice his advances recently. I'm probably fooling myself, but I am actively choosing to believe he's looking out for me as an upperclassman. I am not going to make an assumption with regards to his feelings. I don't encourage anything romantic. I'm only being civil. So…can we please drop it?" She stopped walking and turned towards her companion.

Hajime also stopped.

Reina realised that she was being short with Hajime. She was pushing her frustration about Satoshi to an undeserving man. "Sorry…" she uttered.

Hajime stepped closer and laid both hands on her shoulders. He bent a little so that their eyes were level and smirked. "You don't need to apologise. I think I understand what's going on…but for now, let's let it go. I will say that I don't know him, so I will reserve my judgements. If he gives you trouble, you will come to me, yes?" He waited for Reina to nod before straightening and allowed his arms to fall back to his sides. "Does my youngest brother know? You and Tatsu are attending the same university, right? Does he know?"

Reina looked thoughtful. "Tatsunori and I never talked about Satoshi. At least, I don't think so. I mean…there's not much of a reason. But he does know Satoshi, yes."

Hajime made a mental note to take with his younger brother when he returns from his club's training camp. He gave Reina a nod and changed the subject. "What's this he said about graduate school?"

"It's something I have been considering. I've gotten all the information I need if I do eventually decide to go."

"Satoshi seems to think it's a done deal."

"Don't get me wrong, Hajime," Reina replied as she started walking again, "I am determined to get my masters. Right now, given how things are, I'm considering whether to push for the next school year or postpone until the year after."

Hajime took a moment to digest what she was telling him. "You're taking the literature course at KYU, right? Mom was really proud when she mentioned that you got accepted."

Reina blushed a little but gave a nod. "I've decided to concentrate on Japanese language and literature. Speaking of language and literature—going through Dad's business plan got me thinking of possibly adding more."

"What did you have in mind?"

"Grandfather's suggestion of afternoon tea got me thinking. I haven't really fully figured it out, so I'd like to hear your opinion." Reina paused. "You've noticed that we are getting more and more foreign visitors in this area. What if in addition to the typical afternoon tea experience, we offer to share some of our traditional literature? We can offer it in Japanese for locals like us or Japanese tourists. We could also offer it in English at a different time for foreigners."

"How's your English proficiency?"

"And that's actually why I'm thinking of postponing my graduate school application. I wanted to improve my skills. I can say they're passable but for a more fluent, detailed discussion, I'll need to improve."

Hajime didn't comment right away. Reina grew more and more anxious the longer Hajime stayed silent. She started to feel that perhaps it was a silly suggestion.

Just before Reina could tell him to forget about it, Hajime said, "What if we prepare the sweets and tea during the narration of the story? We could perform the steps of the traditional tea ceremony, or create our own procedure based on it. We can talk about the merits of which we would be preparing first, the tea or the sweets. Or, even at the same time." He allowed his imagination to run free based on her comments.

That stopped Reina short. He was taking her seriously. She thought about his suggestion and a smile slowly formed on her lips. "It would be great too if we make sweets related to the story we're telling."

Hajime grinned. "That would certainly satisfy Mr. Maruyama's concerns about sharing traditions in a fresh way. And if we are taking into consideration the timeline you are setting for yourself with grad school, the renovations won't take a year. If you want to take the year off to improve your English, we can implement the afternoon tea plans in stages. The renovations will take approximately five to six months. So that will leave us six months to see how the plan works. We will have a more solid idea about what works and what needs to be improved on. At the same time, we could also start introducing the special afternoon tea to the public, both in Japanese and English. We would be able to tell if the public is open to the idea or not and adjust accordingly."

"Perhaps when we do start it, we will offer it once a month. It might be a good idea have the events coincide with historical festivals here in Kyoto. It will give us time to prepare and advertise. Not to mention, since it will be coinciding with the festivals, it will give people an extra cultural experience," Reina suggested.

"I like that," said Hajime. They had arrived in front of Reina's apartment. "Are you doing anything tomorrow? Since we aren't needed at the shop, we could prepare a complete plan before we can show your grandparents."

"I'll be doing my thesis in the morning, but you can come over so we can work on it. I'll just be revising some parts of my thesis anyway. I'm actually almost done."

Hajime waited for Reina to open her door before saying, "I'll stop by tomorrow morning at eight. I'll bring breakfast."

***

1860, First year of Man'en, Edo Period

Riku had been able to secure a new home for him and his family. Unfortunately, that quickly depleted the little money they had. It made it impossible to set up his home and establish his shop at two different locations. *The trauma from their hometown was fresh, so he held a thin thread of hope that he could provide his family a house that would be away from the store for extra safety. But financially, he already knew it wasn't feasible, so both he and his wife agreed to set up the new store at the front of their new home.*

Spring was on the cusp of starting. Buds started to sprout on cherry blossom trees. Riku wanted to take advantage of hanami—the annual tradition of cherry blossom viewing. It would be perfect for business, and that was besides its poignant significance that year.

Riku had gone shopping with Shiori earlier. It was challenging to budget for groceries, but ultimately, Riku decided to try to get as many ingredients as he could for namagashi and sakura mochi. Although he wouldn't be able to buy dried cherry blossom leaves, Riku had already started planning how could adjust while still serving the sweets as close to the traditional sakura mochi as possible.

Shiori supported her husband's decision by simply buying rice and spring onions. It would be enough for them both for a while. She also bought the cheapest futon she could find and a single pot. They only had enough left for a single bowl after the other basic kitchen utensils were bought. Riku had been fortunate to still have his work tools; when the attack happened, he had been on his way home and planned to do some maintenance on them.

Riku's heart broke for his young wife. She was also doing her best and was not complaining. He resolved to buy her more bowls and chopsticks when he made more money. For the moment, they were thankful to have a roof over their heads and enough to eat and start their business.

With Kouki on his mother's back, secured in his baby carrier, shopping was done, and the small family headed home.

Days passed but business had been slow. The Maruyama couple was happy for every customer that bought something from them, bowing to them in welcome, thanks, and farewell when they left. They had become more acquainted with their new town. They also had been able to make new friends and acquaintances.

But as an out-of-town Japanese confection master, no matter how beautifully crafted his pieces were, the locals preferred to visit long-established Kyoto stores. While the Maruyamas were one of the best craftsmen in Shinano Province, it didn't hold much weight in Kyoto.

Riku and Shiori noticed that their first customers were those who had travelled the Nakasendo highway and had passed their small village. A very small number of these frequent travellers had been regular customers. Some even expressed their surprise to find the Maruyama couple there in Kyoto. All who knew them from Shinano had mourned when they found out the news of what had happened to that small village.

Riku and Shiori were extremely grateful that they had continued to be their clientele in Kyoto. It might have been a small number of people, but the loyalty of their customers was like a balm to soothe their loss.

It was a painstakingly slow process to build their name in Kyoto, but the couple was determined to persevere in honour of all those who didn't survive, and for their family. The Maruyama name had a long history. Riku and Shiori were going to make sure it continued despite the horrid massacre that had reduced their once beloved village into nothing.

CHAPTER 5

Reina and Hajime were enjoying an ice cream cone while relaxing on a park bench. It was such a nice day with a lot of people enjoying being outdoors. Having spent the whole day working hard on their proposal, they decided to take a leisurely walk around Kyoto before heading to dinner and to the Maruyama ancestral house.

"I'll be heading to Osaka tomorrow," Hajime remarked as he finished his ice cream. Reina turned to look at him. "My best friend is getting married."

"Is Eito still your best friend?" He looked at her in surprise, to which Reina raised an eyebrow. "Hey! Don't look at me like that! You were always with Eito before I left for Tokyo. You two were the ones who almost always came to the shop to buy whatever Mrs. Yoshida ordered. She always said that you two were like two peas in a pod."

Hajime gave out a short laugh. He could remember those days. They had gone to the same schools from elementary all the way to high school. They both left Kyoto after their high school graduation. Hajime headed to France while Eito headed to Osaka.

Having finished her ice cream, Reina stood up and looked at Hajime. "In that case, I'm going to a stationery store and the bank." Hajime frowned as he too stood. Reina smiled and shook her head. *Men.* "I want to give Eito and his new wife a wedding gift so I'm buying a goshugi-bukuro envelope, obviously. I'm sure the financial gift will help them in some way. But I do know it's important to put in new bills as the goshugi. I don't have that much cash on me so let's drop by the bank too."

"You don't have to, you know." He commented as he started following her towards the closest store.

"I know. It's been years since I've heard about Eito, but regardless, he was nice to me growing up. He did go out of his way to protect Tatsu, and I from bullies. The least I could do is wish him well in his marriage." Reina explained.

A sudden memory suddenly came back to Hajime's. He had come down with the flu sometime in junior high school. His youngest brother, Tatsunori, had come home and told them over dinner that when he and Reina were coming home from elementary school, there were some older kids who started harassing them. He was only six at the time. Reina, a year older, tried to stand up to the bullies. But they were also bigger and older than her. Eito was walking home after football club when he happened upon the scene. Without much thought, he drove the bullies away and walked Reina and Tatsunori home.

Reina and Tatsunori had always walked home together since they went to the same school. Tatsunori had to stay a bit late for some reason, but Reina had waited for him. After that incident, Eito made sure to try to check up on them when he could. There wasn't much he could do since the bullies were apparently about a year or two older than Reina but in the same elementary school. Nothing serious ever happened, but the bullies did try to intimidate them until eventually they grew bored and stopped.

It didn't take long to buy a goshugi-bukuro and withdraw the money, which she carefully enclosed. Reina wrote her name on the envelope and handed it to Hajime. "Please also wish him and his new wife a happy marriage for me."

"Of course," Hajime answered as he accepted the plastic. "Do you want anything from Osaka?"

**

Eito was waiting at Shin-Osaka station, and Hajime's train was due to arrive in a few minutes. The last time they saw each other was when Hajime had arrived from France a few months back. Eito had been one of the first people to know that his best friend was planning to move back home. In fact, he highly encouraged him to do it after what Hajime went through.

He was so lost in thought that he didn't notice Hajime walk up to him until he heard, "Eito."

"Hey! How's Kyoto?" Eito greeted as he turned towards Hajime.

Hajime grinned. "Kyoto is like usual this time of year. Are you planning on visiting soon?"

Eito nodded. "We will be there in December just before the new year. Sayaka and I will stay until around January 2 before heading to Nara to visit her family. Then, we will return here."

"That's surprisingly organised this early."

Eito started laughing as they walked up to the ticket machine so Hajime could buy his train ticket.

"By the way, Eito, you do remember Reina Maruyama, right?" Hajime asked.

"Yes, of course! How is she?"

As soon as Hajime got his ticket, the two of them started walking to the platform to take the train to Osaka station. "She's doing great. She's about to graduate university and sent a goshugi for you. I'll hand it over to the receptionist tomorrow."

Eito couldn't help but smile. "She has always been a sweet girl. Graduating? Wow! Time flies!"

"It sure does." Getting on the train, Hajime continued, "I was thinking of getting her something from here."

Nudging Hajime's side with a sly grin, Eito said, "Are you finally moving on, my friend?"

"Rei's just a friend."

"I did tell you that it was okay to start opening up to someone again, to take a chance again."

"That's not the issue. We're just working together now. That's all."

Eito raised an eyebrow but didn't comment, though his expression spoke loud and clear. *Whatever you say, Hajime.* He knew that moving back to Kyoto opened new doors for his friend, and he had a feeling that Hajime's reconnection with Reina was something extra special. He just had a good feeling about it. Or perhaps it was because he was getting married the next day that he couldn't help but be happy and feel positively about everything.

***

"I'm sorry I'm late," Reina said as she sat down in front of her best friend, breathless. She and Aika agreed to meet at the cafe near the station twenty minutes earlier.

Aika put down her phone and looked at her best friend. She pushed her glass of water towards her. Reina bowed in thanks and took the glass

"Problem at city hall?" asked Aika.

Reina nodded. "I submitted some of the documents grandfather asked me to drop off, but the clerk I talked with had more questions. Plus, there were surprisingly a lot of people there today." She looked over the menu. "Oh! They have a new sandwich?"

"Yeah. I saw the same thing earlier and was thinking of trying it."

"Hmm. I think I'll try it too. It looks good!"

After giving their orders, the two settled down again. Aika had been out of Kyoto for the majority of the summer season. She had gone to visit her older sister up north in Hokkaido. Her sister had just given birth, so Aika had gone with their mother to meet the baby. They had stayed for a few weeks to help while her sister recovered. Both had returned to Kyoto just before the obon season – the combination of the ancient belief of ancestral spirits and the

Japanese Buddhist custom of honouring the spirits of ancestors - celebrations.

"How's your sister and the baby?" Reina asked.

Aika handed Reina a souvenir, then scrolled through her photos before handing her phone over. Reina started cooing at the images.

"They are doing okay. My sister had a long labour since it was her first birth. Mom said it was normal for a first baby. Aoi is so cute! I miss her already."

"She is cute," Reina commented as she returned her friend's phone. "She kind of looks like your sister."

"Right? That's also what I said!" Aika exclaimed. "But enough about that…what's this I hear about you running all around Kyoto with a handsome man."

Reina's cheeks heated up, the table suddenly more interesting to look at than her friend's face. "It's not what you think."

Aika raised an eyebrow and leaned forward. "You do know you're blushing like crazy, right?"

Reina's gaze suddenly shot up to her best friend. She could tell Aika was struggling to stop herself from smiling. "Do you remember when I told you I grew up close to a family with four boys?"

"Yes?"

"You know Tatsu. He's the youngest brother. Well, the one before him, Hajime, is working with us at the shop."

"Are you sure it's only a professional and brotherly relationship you have with Tetsunori's older brother?" Aika teased.

Reina frowned and tilted her head. "Huh? Well, we are friends and grew up mostly together before we started working together. I don't think either one of us has ever insinuated or acted otherwise."

Aika leaned back against her chair and crossed her arms. "I bumped into Satoshi and Kai yesterday. Where do you think I heard the news from? Satoshi didn't seem pleased seeing another man walking with you at night. Satoshi is giving off an impression that it was a rather 'romantic' nightly walk."

Reina's frown deepened. "Well, Hajime and I encountered Satoshi a couple of nights ago, so they did meet each other. Hajime was walking me home. But why would Satoshi be bothered? It's not his business. It's not like we are together."

"You and Satoshi, or, you and Hajime?" Aika asked pointedly.

Heat crawled up Reina's neck and turned a darker red. She knew what her best friend was alluding to. She wasn't that dense. "I'm not in a relationship with either of them. Besides, I really don't see Satoshi in that way. You know that."

"But you do see Hajime that way?"

"Okay. I admit I had a slight childhood crush on him," Reina began. But that was a long time ago. I respect the man he became. I like how comfortable it is to talk with him even though we haven't seen each other for a long time. That part hasn't changed much. We work together. That's it."

"You protest too much."

Before any more comments could be made, their orders were served.

CHAPTER 6

Reina and Aika were walking near the train station when they heard someone call out to Reina. Both women turned and saw a man approach, rolling his suitcase behind him.

Reina smiled as she turned fully. "Good afternoon, Hajime. How was the wedding yesterday?"

Aika stared at her best friend before looking back at the man. When Reina said that he was one of Tatsunori's older brothers, Aika had a vague image in mind. She could see the family resemblance, but Hajime had a different air about him. While Tatsunori had this boyish charm that endeared him to a lot of women around their university, Hajime was charismatic in a different way.

Tall and well-built. Black hair with hazel eyes. There was a certain confidence in him that Tatsunori was still growing into. The gentleness of his gaze towards her best friend, though, made her think there was more to the relationship than Reina was prepared to admit. She would even hazard a guess that her dear best friend didn't know, or perhaps telling herself, not to look beyond their established labels. Looking at the man in the flesh made Aika realise what Reina might've found attractive about Hajime in the past, and perhaps why she was stopping herself from being attracted now.

Hajime grinned, lifted the paper bag he was holding, and offered it to Reina.

Reina tilted her to the side in question before hesitantly reaching for the bag. "For me?"

Hajime nodded in reply.

"Can I open it now?"

Another nod.

She bowed in thanks and opened the bag. A big smile graced her features; she couldn't help it. She took out the bear wearing a graduation gown and cap. It was too cute not to appreciate. She then hugged the bear close. "Thank you so much, Hajime."

"You're welcome, but there's something else inside the bag."

"You really didn't have to get me anything."

"The one in the bag is from Eito and his new wife," he clarified

Reina retrieved a small white box with a pink and purple plum obi ornament inside. "Oh, it's so beautiful. Tell me when you send a thank you card. I'll send mine as well." She put all the items back into the bag everything and then it dawned on her. "Oh! Where are my manners?" She looked up at Hajime, "I'd like to introduce you to my best friend, Aika Harada."

Aika stepped forward and bowed. "Nice to meet you. I'm Aika Harada. You must be Hajime Yoshida. Rei was telling me so much about you."

Reina blushed as Hajime bowed and returned his sentiments.

"Anyway, I'll leave Reina with you, okay? I just received a message from my boyfriend asking me to dinner." She gave Reina a look and bowed again towards Hajime before walking off.

Hajime and Reina looked at each other. She gave him a sheepish smile. "I'm sorry about her."

Hajime gave a short laugh and placed a hand on her back to urge her to start walking. "No problem. I have a best friend too."

Reina laughed alongside him.

"They're crazy," They both said together and started laughing more.

A companionable silence enveloped them even as people bustled around. Locals and tourists alike were everywhere. At four in the afternoon, the streets of Kyoto were still busy.

They were walking in front of a set of stores when something caught Reina's eye. She stopped walking and looked at the books displayed in the front window.

Hajime noticed her pause and walked back a couple of steps to see what she was looking at. "Do you want to go inside?"

"No, that's okay," Reina answered, shaking her head. She then looked up at him sheepishly and added, "Sorry. The book I'm waiting for hasn't been released yet. Some of the books do look interesting, but I'll check it out some other time."

"Are you sure? It's fine to go in since we are already here anyway."

"Checking out books is never a short event for me." She laughed as she started to walk away.

"So that part of you hasn't changed either," Hajime commented as he walked beside her. She looked up at him curiously, which made him chuckle. "When you were really little, I'd often see you on your dad's lap while he read a book to you during afternoons when we'd visit the shop. You two would be at a corner table and he'd be reading a storybook. My parents found it really amusing that when your parents would ask what you'd want for your birthday, you'd always say a book."

Reina blushed. It was true, though. "I do remember there was one New Year our families spent together. I think my parents were going to help your parents with the preparations for the first temple visit of the year. Thinking about it now as an adult, it wasn't surprising my parents helped with the preparations for hatsumode. It is a lot of work! I do remember experiencing hatsumode a little differently that New Year. To be honest, my memories of that day aren't much but what I do remember was sitting with Tatsu under the kotatsu while you and Masashi read the story of the legend of Kasajizou to us. I think I was around six or seven at the time. Itsuki was helping the adults."

Hajime remembered too. It was the last year when things seemed to be normal and…happy. She was seven at the time, and it was a few months later, after her birthday, that her father's health started declining.

Unconsciously, his grip on his luggage tightened. His eyes grew softer with nostalgia. A sigh filled with different emotions – longing, regret, guilt, and, appreciation - escaped his lips. "To be honest, those were the kind of memories that made me homesick when I was in France," Hajime said.

Reina glanced at him. Her voice was soft when she finally replied, "I thought you'd come back earlier…to visit at least."

Hajime sighed. Looking back, he should have done a lot of things differently, but it was no use thinking about it like that. Nothing can change the past. He wouldn't be the person he was now if he didn't have the past he had.

"There were a lot of things, Rei—a lot of reasons that might not even make sense now. Not all the decisions I made were good, apparently, but if I'd chosen differently then, I wouldn't be here now." He looked at her and gave a soft smile. "It's true that I could have avoided a lot of things, especially the bad ones. But no matter how I contemplate 'what-ifs' or 'could have been', I will never be able to change the past. I choose to believe everything works out to be as it's meant to be."

Reina considered his answer. Bad things…she couldn't help but be wonder what he meant but felt like she shouldn't ask. She decided to smile back. "Yes, you're here now, Hajime." Her smile widened as she grabbed his arm and added, "You still owe me some stories about France. I'll even treat you to dinner."

Hajime quickly let go of his suitcase and grabbed Reina's arm to stop her from walking. "How about this," he bargained as she looked up at him and waited. "How about I drop off my stuff at my apartment real quick. You can leave your stuff too. Then, we go buy groceries and I make you my favourite French dish? How does that sound?"

He could see the excitement enter her eyes. "Really? You're really going to let me try your favourite dish?"

Hajime laughed as he reached for his suitcase and started leading her towards his new apartment. "I'll even tell you the struggle I had learning how to cook it." Her twinkling laughter sounded behind him, keeping the smile on his face.

Before they could go far, both of them heard their names being called, then turned to see Hajime's eldest brother and his wife.

"Haruka!" Reina smiled and bowed at the older woman as the couple got closer. "It's been a while!"

"Itsuki," Hajime greeted his oldest brother who simply replied, "Hajime,"

Reina turned to Itsuki while Hajime faced his brother's wife. "Haruka, how are you today?" Hajime said.

Itsuki opened his arms and gave Reina a bear hug. "Hi, Rei."

Reina returned his hug, then looked up and answered, "Hi Itsuki."

"What are you two up to?" Itsuki asked as he stepped by his wife and laid a hand on the small of her back.

"Hajime offered to cook and let me try his favourite French dish," Reina replied excitedly.

"You both are free to join us if you like. We just need to buy the groceries before I can start cooking," Hajime offered.

Haruka and Itsuki looked at each other in a silent exchange between husband and wife. Then, Itsuki finally answered, "Sure. We're bringing dessert then. Your apartment, Hajime?" At his younger brother's nod, he added, "We will see you there in about an hour then?"

"That will be enough time. See you later! Come on, Rei."

Reina bowed towards the couple and jogged to catch up with Hajime.

The couple looked at each other again in another quiet exchange.

***

Dinner had been full of laughs and stories. Hajime regaled them with his time in France, including some embarrassing tales about language barriers.

Itsuki felt relieved. It had been a long time since he saw his younger brother this carefree and full of laughter. This was the brother he remembered before he left to study in France. The one who returned a few months ago had been more reserved, quiet, and closed off. There was rage behind his younger brother's eyes that he would only get a glimpse of. It would quickly be covered or hidden behind a mask Hajime had worn around all of them. Hajime had always been kind and polite. That had never changed but there were a lot of subtle body language that told Itsuki his younger brother had a darkness within him that he was hiding. As the eldest brother, Itsuki could tell that the man who returned was different from the one who'd left.

While it was to be expected that Hajime would change during his time away, Itsuki often saw the hurt, instead of the rage, that flashed through Hajime's eyes before he'd disguise the pain with a stoic expression or a polite smile. Itsuki wasn't sure what he could do, but he hoped for the best. From what Itsuki could tell, Hajime's rekindling bond with Reina was doing him good.

Out of everyone in his family, he was the one Hajime had the most contact with while he was away. Every month from the moment Hajime started his part-time job as a student until he lost his last job, Hajime would send Itsuki whatever money he could spare to invest. Since Itsuki had finished accounting with the intention of managing the shrine—the duties would be officially passed on to him—he had also become the family's financial advisor. He would make sure that no matter what, every single member of his family was financially stable.

Hajime would tell him some of the things that were going on with him and often asked for his advice. Itsuki was privy to information their parents weren't. He knew the details about what happened at Hajime's previous job and the sudden end of his romantic relationship. He was also privy to Hajime's arrest and subsequent release. Their parents and other brothers got the sanitised version. Still, it was difficult to see the change in his brother the moment he got back to Japan. Nothing could have prepared Itsuki for it.

It was difficult to stop the relieved smile that snuck up on Itsuki's lips as he witnessed how things were at the moment. Itsuki was so lost in his thoughts that he almost missed Hajime's comment.

"I can't believe I'm saying this, but months after the fact and after much reflection, being home has made me realise that I'm actually grateful things happened the way they did."

"What do you mean?" Itsuki asked reflexively. He wasn't even sure he'd asked the question.

Hajime looked his older brother in the eyes to let him know how completely serious he was. "Sure, it was frustrating to undergo work politics, being blamed for things I never did, punished. It was also beyond aggravating to be arrested by the police and jailed for baseless accusations. The workplace I once loved became so toxic. I was forced out…among other things. I was angry and bitter about it, but now, I understand that it needed to happen or else I wouldn't have come home."

Itsuki reached out and laid a hand on his brother's shoulder. "I, for one, am glad you came home. It was infuriating that I couldn't do much for you while you were carrying this burden, but you came out stronger for it."

***

After helping clean up, Itsuki, Haruka, and Reina headed towards the entrance door. Hajime followed.

"We can walk Rei home, Hajime. It's fine." Itsuki offered.

Reina nodded. "You're already home, Hajime. Plus, you just came back from Osaka. You must be tired. I'll be fine."

Hajime ushered everyone out the door and locked it. "Granted you two live two stops away from Rei, you don't have to trouble yourselves. I can walk Rei home."

"I can find my way home, Hajime," Reina tried to put her two cents in.

"Of course, you can, Rei, but it's getting late. Please, for this old man's peace of mind," he teased, pulling her along towards the staircase.

She scoffed and replied, "You're not old."

He laughed and ruffled her hair.

He then looked to see the amused expressions on his brother and sister-in-law's faces, who were quietly walking behind the pair. "Don't worry. I can make sure this squirt doesn't get into trouble."

Reina exclaimed, "Hey!" and elbowed him on his abdomen, causing Hajime to laugh again.

Itsuki shook his head, laid an arm around each of Hajime and Reina's shoulders and started walking them out of the building and towards the train station, his amused wife following them.

"What am I going to do about you two?" Itsuki playfully sighed, causing the two to laugh. It was times like this that made Itsuki feel like he had four younger siblings instead of three. But then again, the Yoshida brothers had always been close to Reina. His family treated her as one of them. So, having four younger siblings wasn't really far from the truth.

***

Reina and Hajime separated from them at her stop. Haruka looked up at her husband and said, "It's nice to see Hajime laughing again."

Itsuki couldn't help but smile. He gave a nod before answering, "I know what you mean. This time…they were real smiles too."

Haruka hooked her arm with her husband's and looked up at him. "This is the first time I've seen Hajime interact with Rei."

He met his wife's gaze. "What's your impression?"

She smiled. "Are you sure there isn't something there?"

He chuckled as he looked towards where they were walking. It seemed like those two were in a deep conversation, but he could feel the weight of his wife's gaze. "Those two have always been close, closer than perhaps Rei and Tatsu. Though I'm sure you didn't miss the gentleness in both their gazes. Perhaps there is something there. If there was, I wouldn't object to it. I'm actually hoping there is. I'll probably even encourage it."

CHAPTER 7

Tatsunori was relieved to be home. Even though his club's training camp was exciting, it was hard work. School was about to start next Monday, so it would be great to relax for a few days before then.

"I'm home," he called out as soon as he stepped into the house. He couldn't help but smile. The moment he opened the door, the smell of his mother's baking greeted him.

"Welcome home, Tatsu," she replied.

Tatsunori walked further into the house, following his nose to the kitchen. "Something smells good, Mom."

Yuuka smiled warmly towards her youngest son. "Rei's uncle is coming home today. I'm baking some of his favourite apple crumble pie."

"That's great! Does that mean he's okay now?"

"Mrs. Maruyama said that the doctors still advise him not to work. He will be starting rehabilitation next week and will need to relearn how to use the left part of his body." His mother went back to her pies. "I'll be heading to Amai Omoide in a few minutes if you want to tag along."

"Okay." He then turned towards the hallway leading to his room. "I'll just leave my bags in my room. I'll help you with the pies, Mom."

***

"Welcome!"

The greeting came automatically as soon as Tatsunori opened the door of Amai Omoide, then held it for his mother while carrying a basket full of pies for her. It was near closing time when they entered, but there were still quite a few customers inside.

Sayaka and Mio were the ones manning the front of the store. Both smiled when they realised who'd entered.

"Good afternoon." Both Yuuka and Tatsunori offered a greeting bow. Yuuka then asked, "Are Hajime and Rei here?"

The older woman bowed and returned the greeting. "Yes. Both of them are busy preparing tomorrow morning's batches. We are about to close in fifteen minutes. Would you like me to call either of them?"

Yuuka shook her head. "We will wait for closing time. Don't mind us. We will just sit at one of the tables." She then ushered her youngest.

While waiting, Mio came over with a tray. She set down a cup of barley tea for each of them.

"Oh, Ms. Fujiwara, you didn't need to—" Yuuka started.

Mio cut her off with a smile and a shake of her head. "It's no trouble, Mrs. Yoshida."

"Thank you, Ms. Fujiwara," Toshinori said as he took his cup. He then looked towards his mother, "Mom—"

Before Tatsunori could start what he wanted to say, they heard Hajime's voice.

"Mom, Tatsu..." Yuuka and Tatsunori looked towards the curtain. "Mrs. Ito told us you two were here."

"You didn't have to come out to meet us, Hajime. We could have waited until you and Rei were done with work," Yuuka reprimanded.

Her son smiled and shook his head. "We're finished, actually. We're just doing inventory since construction will be starting next week. Rei shooed me out here." Hajime couldn't help but chuckle. "She said I should greet the two of you, and she has everything handled. But anyway, we'll start bringing some of the equipment to the Maruyama house tonight and then grab the rest over the weekend."

"I'd be glad to help, Brother. Do you need me to get the van?" Tatsunori offered.

Hajime nodded. "Could you take out the supplies we usually keep at the back? We will need as much space as we can manage."

"Got it. I'll be right back." Tatsunori then headed back home.

Hajime turned to his mother. "Sorry to leave you for a bit, Mom. I'll just let Rei know."

***

"Okay, that's about all the equipment we can transport for the day," Hajime commented as he closed the back of the van.

"We can start carrying the tables now, Hajime," Mio said as she and Sayaka waited for instruction to proceed.

They decided to transport everything they could to the Maruyama house for storage. In the meantime, they'd continue the sweets production on a smaller scale and take made-to-order requests. For the duration of the renovations, Amai Omoide would function like a home-based business, just like how it started in the 1860s.

"You can go ahead with Rei," Hajime said, which prompted Reina to tap Tatsunori's shoulder to ask for the keys. "Tatsunori and I will deal with the tables. You two can help Rei unload." The two ladies nodded and got in the van.

Before Reina could walk towards the driver's seat, Hajime reached out to stop her. "Wait for us, Rei. Tatsu and I will be there with a table before you all finish unloading."

"Are you sure you don't want to wait until I get back to help with the tables?"

Hajime smirked and laid a hand on top of Reina's head. "We'll see you in a little while." While Reina got into the driver's seat, he turned towards his brother. "Ready?"

Tatsunori nodded.

Before they left, Yuuka said, "I'll call your dad over. We will arrange the remaining tables and chairs to make it easier for you all later."

It took a few trips, but eventually, they finished transferring everything. Hajime and Reina stayed behind while Tatsunori drove the last batch of chairs and tables together with the Yoshida parents, Issei and Yuuka. Sayaka and Mio had already started helping the elderly Maruyama couple arrange everything at the house. Yuuka had volunteered to prepare dinner for all of them after she was told that Kouji and Yuzuki planned to order dinner. Reina and Hajime wanted to make sure nothing was missed before they too joined the others at the Maruyama residence. Reina double-checked everything behind the counter while Hajime took one last glance in the kitchen.

"All good in here?" Reina asked as she set the curtain aside and walked into the kitchen. Hajime took one last sweep before ushering her out and turning off the lights.

Reina looked around the almost empty store. A sense of nostalgia came over her. She grew up here. Memories of her father were especially poignant. While she would miss how things were, she was also excited for the changes they'd initiated. But looking at the partial emptiness of the store was somehow chipping away at the walls she had wrapped around her heart. It was like reality was slowly catching up now that she had a moment to be still and take it all in.

She felt a hand settle on her right shoulder. Reina looked up. She could tell by Hajime's gaze that he could guess what she was thinking about.

No words were exchanged. Hajime gently pulled her to him and wrapped his arms around her. He could always tell when her emotions were threatening to overwhelm her. The past weeks had been tough, and despite her smiles, Hajime knew that her uncle's stroke had unearthed memories from when her father was dying, reigniting new fears.

Reina closed her eyes. She allowed the steady rhythm of Hajime's heart to calm her raging emotions. After a moment, she wrapped her arms around him.

"Do you want to talk about it?" Hajime whispered. When Reina shook her head, Hajime tightened his embrace.

Both remained in each other's arms for a while. There weren't any words needed. Hajime offered a quiet comfort that Reina welcomed.

When Reina regained control of the torrent inside her, she loosened her hold, but he didn't. As Reina looked up, her breath caught. A warmth and gentleness that she'd never seen from Hajime shone from his eyes. Hear rushed to her face.

Hajime lifted his hand to cup Reina's cheek, and her blush deepened. A soft smile spread across his lips. "Know that you don't need to hide or pretend. If it gets too overwhelming, I'm always here for you,"

When Hajime laid a kiss on her forehead, Reina breathlessly whispered his name.

***

Hajime saw the fear and uncertainty on Reina's face. He could very well read the thoughts and emotions going through her head. He wanted to take it all away if he could.

Ever since they were young, he had always had a strong urge to look out for her. When they were children, it felt more like a brother looking after a younger sibling. Regardless, he had always held her in high regard. These past months, working closely and getting to know each other again, Hajime hadn't wanted to admit what was taking shape between them.

When Eito hinted at something more to his relationship with Reina, Hajime opposed the idea. If he was being honest, there was a part of him that didn't believe his immediate dismissal of Eito's suggestion. Part of him felt confused, and he reflected on his reaction privately. He continued to do so until after his trip.

Hajime couldn't deny that his heart leapt when he had come home from Osaka. It leapt some more when he saw Reina's reaction to his small gift. As the weeks passed, it became more and more difficult to deny his growing attraction to her. He hesitated because he didn't want to presume anything, and he most definitely didn't want to lose their bond. He would never want her to feel awkward in his presence. Hajime also wanted to be absolutely sure about what he was feeling; he didn't want to treat her as a rebound.

There was also a fear that permeated in Hajime's heart and mind. There was a darkness that he hadn't fully purged from his being. He didn't want to subject Reina to it. She became one of his motivations in fighting the darkness. He had started to seek professional help soon after he got back from Osaka.

In that moment inside Amai Omoide and just behind the counter, Hajime's instincts told him to comfort Reina. It felt right when he brought her into his arms, and he resolved to keep treating her as he always had. He would support her no matter what he felt. But when she looked up at him and her face bloomed red, he took the risk of letting her know how he truly felt.

"Know that you don't need to hide or pretend. If it gets too overwhelming, I'm always here for you."

He kissed her forehead and heard her breathlessly call his name, that one utterance carrying so much with it.

Hajime made sure to resume eye contact before saying, "I like you, Reina." He watched her eyes fill with tenderness. "I'm not expecting you to return my feelings, nor will I pressure you into anything." He wanted to say more but stopped when she laid her hand atop his, still cupping her cheek.

"I actually had a crush on you when I was younger," Reina admitted, her face growing warmer again, the memory of her childhood infatuation still a little embarrassing.

Hajime was amused by her reaction. Even if she didn't realise it, she was adorable when she blushed. He gently lifted her chin with a finger.

"I…" Reina hesitated, then took a breath to give herself more courage. "Ever since we reunited, I didn't want to allow myself to feel anything more."

Hajime nodded in understanding—had done the very same.

"Is it…is it really okay to like you back? I don't have to stop myself?" Reina asked.

"Will you be willing to take the risk with me, Reina? Will you be with me?"

Reina gave him a shy smile. "Yes, Hajime."

It was then that they shared their first kiss.

***

As soon as Hajime finished locking the entrance, they heard Tatsunori call out to them. They noticed that he was carrying a bag of ice.

"Mom asked me to buy some ice," Tatsunori offered.

"Is there anything else we need to get while we are out?" Reina asked as she and Hajime started walking towards the Maruyama house with Tatsunori.

Tatsunori shook his head, then noticed Hajime and Reina's linked fingers. "Can I say though—it's about time, you two."

Reina ducked her head as she blushed, and Hajime squeezed her hand in reassurance.

"So, you've been waiting for this *I-told-you-so* moment, then?" Hajime replied in amusement.

Tatsunori laughed good naturedly. "As the youngest brother, I only get a few chances like this in a lifetime, so I'm taking it, Hajime."

This prompted Hajime to laugh and Reina to simply shake her head. She let out an amused huff.

"But seriously, though," Tatsunori started, then waited until he had Hajime and Reina's complete attention. "I'm really happy that this finally happened." His smile was genuine. "Don't worry, Hajime. I'll watch out for Reina more now on campus. Satoshi might finally realise that Reina is not for him." Hajime had sent him a message to ask about Satoshi when he was still at training camp. Tatsunori had called Hajime instead of waiting to get back to answer his older brother's questions. It was obvious to him that Hajime had encountered Satoshi and noticed things himself.

Reina couldn't help the groan that escaped her lips. "Satoshi? I never encouraged anything romantic with him. He certainly doesn't have a say on whom I share a relationship with."

The two brothers shared a look before Hajime replied, "I've only met him once, but those eyes don't lie. He felt threatened because I was there."

Tatsunori nodded. "It's true he helps people whenever someone has academic issues. Even I'll admit he's brilliant. There is no denying that he's very intelligent. His academic achievements speak for themselves. But...Hajime is right. The eyes don't lie. You don't see how he looks at you when you aren't paying attention. We had a one-on-one chat one time."

Reina stopped in her tracks. *What?!* "One-on-one chat? Who initiated it?" While she did believe that Satoshi Fujii wasn't a violent person, she still didn't like the idea of any animosity, especially towards anyone she loved. She had been hearing a lot of stories about Satoshi approaching some of her male friends around campus recently. Her friends confirmed having those conversation but never clarified what kind of supposed conversations they were having. Reina tried to pry them for information, but they'd only tell her that Satoshi warned them off against her. They never revealed specific details, telling them that they handled it – told Satoshi off mostly. Unanimously, every single one of them told her to forget about it.

Reina was reaching the limits of her tolerance of Satoshi's behaviour. This thing with Tatsunori might just push her over the edge.

She knew that if it were Tatsunori who initiated the talk, he would have been pushed, thinking it was necessary. She knew Tatsunori well enough that his easy-going nature would take a back seat if he thought someone he considered family or friend was threatened. If Satoshi was the one who initiated it, Reina would definitely have something to say about it. She had always been protective of Tatsunori since they were children. It wasn't going to stop now that they were adults.

Tatsunori shrugged. "It's not that important, Rei." He smiled again. "Let's just say that he learned to be cordial towards me because he realised I wasn't backing down." Reina was an honorary member of his family, regardless of blood. He would do anything for family. Now that she and Hajime had come out with their relationship, he had all the more reason to look out for her. She was his sister no matter what anyone says.

"Aw, Tatsu…" Reina gave him a side hug and kissed his cheek. The blush that broke out on his face was adorable. "As long as you didn't get hurt or get in trouble, I'll let it go. Whatever machismo thing that is going on here—I believe you when you say it isn't important. You're the coolest younger brother ever."

Tatsunori snorted. He started elbowing Reina and mock-whispered, "Now, if you could convince Hajime that I'm the coolest, that would be awesome."

All three of them burst out laughing.

Hajime wrapped an arm around Tatsunori's neck as they walked. "Let's get going before the ice melts." Reina chuckled as she followed behind the brothers. In a whisper, Hajime added, "Thank you for looking after her."

"You never needed to ask, Hajime," Tatsunori whispered back.

CHAPTER 8

Reina and Aika were at the university library working on their theses. Neither noticed when Tatsunori walked up to the table.

"Sorry, but do you mind if I share your table?" he whispered as the two looked up.

Aika smiled and gave a nod before turning back to her laptop. Reina also smiled and cleared some of her books out of the way as Tatsunori sat beside her.

"Thank you," he said in a soft voice as he took out his laptop.

All three of them got lost in what they were doing, but after some time, they started hearing some whispered conversations from tables behind them. All three looked at each other.

Aika shook her head, quick to dismiss what was happening. From the moment Tatsunori entered university, a lot of whispers, especially from women, followed him around. It wasn't a surprise. With Tatsunori's friendly and outgoing attitude, he attracted a lot of attention, but he was more than his looks. He was one of the most sought-after bachelors in their university. One of the most 'controversial' things about him in the beginning was his frequent female company - Reina, who was also very attractive. The two could be seen together around campus often and it caused a lot of people to speculate about their relationship. When a brave few asked, both Tatsunori and Reina were open about growing up together and their families were close. While it did settle some speculations, it didn't stop all rumours. Since then, the two would ignore anything they deemed ridiculous and went on their business. Aika had seen and heard it all before, so she decided to concentrate on her work.

Tatsunori and Reina exchanged glances. Reina lifted an eyebrow while Tatsunori shrugged it off. He never did give any effort in listening or acknowledging rumours.

"...you know, Satoshi Fujii, right?"

"Yeah. He's that cute graduate student, right?"

"I heard that Reina isn't really nice. She strung him on and now he's heartbroken. Apparently, Satoshi told a friend of mine when they went out drinking that Reina found herself a boyfriend."

A gasp was heard. "Really? So, she's more than likely playing around with Tatsunori!"

Reina knew whom the voices belonged to. They never liked her because of her close relationship with Tatsunori. They were whom Reina termed as 'Tatsunori's fan girls'. A few months after Tatsunori started at the university, *that* particular pair had approached Reina and started 'warning' Reina away from Tatsunori. Reina had simply raised an eyebrow and excused herself. She shared the incidence with Tatsunori, who wanted to rectify it immediately. Reina talked him out of it, saying it wasn't worth the time since it looked like they wouldn't be listening no matter what was said. She had been proven right a few months after.

The pair made it their mission to confront or harass Reina intermittently. There was one time Reina confronted the pair and in no way was her message unclear. Reina told them there was no way she would ever avoid Tatsunori. She would have said more but Tatsunori had decided to approach them when he noticed Reina talking with the pair. When he was close enough, Tatsunori had placed an arm around Reina's shoulder, horrifying his two fans. He then went on to tell them off, saying that Reina was important to him and he had no qualms on confronting anybody who antagonised her. He then proceeded to drag Reina away.

When they were far enough, Reina had scolded Tatsunori. She told him the impression of his words and his actions. He looked sheepish when he finally realised the validity of what Reina had said. They both then decided to let it go since they couldn't do anything to undo what had been done. They never made their sibling-like relationship a secret. People would catch them calling each other 'brother' or 'sister' but unfortunately, there were still people who proved to be entirely dense.

The pair occupying the table behind them were one of those annoyingly obtuse. Aika had been close to losing her patience more than once against the pair but Reina would always pacify her. She'd remind her best friend that it wasn't worth the effort.

"Shameful, right? I mean look at her now! She's acting as it there's nothing wrong! Breaking someone's heart would have at least make someone feel guilty. Apparently, Reina Maruyama isn't as good as she would like people to believe."

Tatsunori was about to react when Reina patted his hand. "Finish your work, Tatsu." He gave her a sharp look. He didn't like what was going on.

Reina simply smiled and went back to her studies.

Tatsunori bit his tongue and forced himself to concentrate on his assignment. His fingers clenched tightly around his pen when he felt another pat on his hand from Reina. He looked up at her again only to find that her gaze was set on her laptop.

"Rumours are just that. Rumours. No matter how far and wide they reach, it will never make things true. It is enough that we know what's true," Reina whispered.

"Don't think for one minute I'm not aware that they hurt you. I'm not going to stand for that. This has been going on long enough," Tatsunori whispered back.

Reina made eye contact before smiling. "That's the nature of rumours, Tatsu. They intend to hurt one way or another. We can't control that. What I can control is how I choose to react. If the new rumours were indeed started by Satoshi, then he isn't as kind as I thought. Lesson learned. It's laughable to even dignify the idea that I'm toying with you. I'm not going to exert any effort on that."

Tatsunori snorted at that. He did admit that it was ridiculous.

"Fine. If it escalates though, I'm not holding back."

"Fair enough. Oh, by the way, Haruka's birthday is coming up. What are you planning on giving her? I can't think of anything."

Tatsunori smiled sheepishly. Reina knew that look. "Either you forgot, or you're as lost as me,"

"Can I go with the second one?"

"It's more like a combination of the two from the looks of it," Aika commented, finally joining the conversation. "I'm done for the day," she added as she started closing her books and her laptop. "If you guys are done, we could get out of here. We could grab some lunch and start shopping for gifts after. I don't know about you, but the atmosphere here is getting…stale."

Both Reina and Tatsunori knew this was Aika's way of addressing the gossip, so they got to clearing their things from the table and packing up.

"Where did you have in mind?" Reina asked.

"Well, we could head to Kyoto Station. Let's pick a restaurant and then check out the shops nearby. If you guys still don't find anything, we could try some place else. I have to meet up with my boyfriend at one though."

Reina turned to Tatsunori and asked, "Do you have any afternoon classes?"

"I'm done for the day." As soon as Reina nodded in acknowledgement, he changed the subject, "Has Hajime bought a gift yet?"

"I'm meeting him today during his lunch break, around one. We decided to window shop before we both head to work this afternoon."

Aika giggled at the two as she led the way down the stairs, "It certainly looks like it's going to be challenging shopping trip if all three of you haven't got the faintest idea on what to get Haruka."

As they were leaving the building, they ran into Satoshi and a few of his friends.

"Good afternoon, Satoshi, Hayato, Shin." Reina bowed slightly before continuing on. Tatsunori and Aika did the same and kept walking.

Before they got far, Satoshi reached out and grabbed Reina's arm. It was strong enough to make her turn towards him, shock widening her eyes. She hadn't expected him to do that.

"Hey, let her go," Tatsunori immediately said.

"I heard it's true you have a boyfriend. I wasn't imagining the closeness you have with Hajime," Satoshi said, disregarding Tatsunori altogether.

Reina tried to extract her arm, but his grip was firm. "Pardon me for saying this, Satoshi, but it isn't any of your business. My relationships don't concern you."

His grip tightened. "I never took you as someone who leads a person on. You should have just come clean when you introduced Hajime." He spit the word *boyfriend* with barely concealed anger. "I've treated you with respect. Don't I deserve the same curtesy?" He added in an attempt to pacify the situation.

Reina continued to pull on her arm. "Being polite isn't synonymous to being a tease. I never led you on. Let me go, Satoshi." She refused to interact with him further. As far as she was concerned, he wasn't entitled to answers. His behaviour only strengthened her resolve; he was excusing his actions by making them seem like they were her fault. It was blatantly obvious that he was trying to manipulate and control her.

Tatsunori forcefully pulled Satoshi's hand from Reina and positioned himself in front of her. "It's better for you to walk away, Satoshi. There's nothing for you here."

Before Satoshi could do anything, one of his friends, Hayato, said, "She's right. Her decisions and relationships don't concern you. Let it go."

Satoshi glared at him.

Shin sighed. "Regardless of how you feel, Satoshi, Reina was never yours. She's your underclassman. While we do have an obligation to look out for our underclassmen, we don't control them. It certainly doesn't oblige her to reciprocate your romantic intentions." He then started pulling on Satoshi's arm, leading him away from the building.

Hayato bowed towards the remaining three. "Sorry about that, Reina. We will deal with Satoshi. He won't bother you again."

Reina didn't reply but bowed to acknowledge their words. Tatsunori still stood protectively in front of her. He watched the men drag Satoshi away.

"Are you okay, Rei?" Aika asked as she joined Reina's side. Tatsunori turned quickly to judge for himself.

"Shaken, but I'm okay," Reina reassured as she started rubbing the arm Satoshi had grabbed. "I never encouraged anything beyond simple courtesy."

"This is not your fault, Rei. It's all him," Tatsunori insisted.

"I agree, Rei. It's Satoshi who has an issue, not you," Aika offered without preamble.

***

Tatsunori, Reina and Aika shared ideas on what they thought constituted to a perfect gift while walking from the station. After what happened at campus, Reina didn't want to talk about it anymore than they already had. She didn't want the incident with Satoshi ruin the rest of their day.

Aika received a message from her boyfriend asking her to meet earlier than planned. She'd contemplated on cancelling in lieu of helping Reina and Tatsunori shop for Haruka. Reina could tell the thoughts that were running through Aika's mind, insisting that it was fine if she needed to leave early.

Hajime joined them near the entrance of the station. Walking up to them, he noticed their expressions. There was a tightness to Tatsunori's shoulders. A hardness that was subtly concealed behind his younger brother's eyes alerted Hajime that there was something that aroused the ire of Tatsunori. No one looking would have guessed given that he was engaging Reina and Aika as if nothing was wrong. Hajime knew better.

As Reina saw Aika off, Hajime turned to his brother and whispered, "Is there something wrong?" His younger brother's lip was set in a line who quietly explained to Hajime what'd happened earlier. Hajime's eyes narrowed as he listened and clenched his jaw tight when his brother recalled how Satoshi had acted. Shifting his gaze towards his girlfriend, Hajime noticed there wasn't any sign suggesting that Reina was distressed.

"I wanted so much to punch Satoshi. It was hard controlling myself." Tatsunori admitted.

"As much as I would have supported you and would have taken a swing of my own, it's good you didn't resort to violence. You'd have receive some tongue-lashing from Reina, I'm sure," Hajime answered.

Tatsunori snorted and commented, "It's over now." Hajime had simply nodded his head in acknowledgement.

"Where do you want to eat?" Hajime asked when he noticed Reina walking towards them.

Reina thought about it before answering, "I think I'd like some tempura for today." As the three headed towards their usual go-to restaurant for tempura, Reina started, "Tatsunori and I have been talking with Aika about gift ideas for Haruka. She gave us suggestions, but Tatsunori and I can't seem to agree on what to get."

Tatsunori promptly snorted. "I was okay with most of Aika's ideas. It was more you, Rei, who didn't seem to think they suit Haruka."

"Tatsu, I love you and all, trust me this is coming from a place of love, little brother, but I seriously think there's something wrong with you if you believe getting her a bath giftset is a nice gift. Aika only said that because you asked if there are toiletry sets that are popular for ladies. I've gone shopping with Haruka and she's very particular with those stuff. I don't recommend going that route." Reina defended.

At Tatsunori's lost look, Hajime started laughing. "I'd listen to Rei with this one, little brother. Unless you know the differences are between conditioners and hair treatment and stuff, I don't recommend considering a bath set as a gift. I have no idea about the differences too! It's safe if we go with other options. Besides, do you know Haruka's scent preferences? Mom used to like flowery scents for her shampoo. Now, she asks me to buy something fruity. I'm sure you've been asked to do the grocery too."

Tatsunori had a thoughtful look. "Yeah. Now that you've mentioned it, you're right."

After having lunch, the trio window shopped for a little while before heading towards Amai Omoide.

When they reached the fork on the road, Tatsunori turned to them, "I'll head home. See you at school tomorrow, Rei?"

Reina hugged Tatsunori and squeezed tight. "Thanks for today, Tatsu. But I won't be seeing you tomorrow," She stepped back. "I'll be spending the rest of the week and the weekend museum-hopping for my thesis, but I'll see you on campus next week."

"Oh! Best wishes! I'll see you when you get back then," Tatsunori commented.

"I'll get you a souvenir from Nara or Tokyo. Let me know if you have any requests while I'm there. I'll get it for you," Reina offered.

"Thanks, sis. I'll do that."

Hajime laid an arm around Reina's shoulder. "We've got to head to work now," He turned to his brother. "See you later, Tatsu,"

His brother gave a nod and headed towards the shrine.

***

The days that followed were busy for Reina, and her family and boyfriend barred her from doing any shop-related work for the next little while. They wanted her to concentrate on her thesis.

She had spent two days at the museum in Kyoto, and before that, the one at Nara. Her last museum visit would be in Tokyo, and she planned to spend the weekend in there to finish her research on national treasures related to calligraphy.

It was about a two-hour trip from Kyoto to Tokyo with the bullet train. Upon leaving Kyoto, she sent a message to her mother to say she'd be in Tokyo over the weekend. There was no reply. Her heart squeezed when she saw that her message had been read.

Reina sighed. She decided to keep her phone and looked out the window, getting lost inside her head. Her thoughts drifted to Hajime. A part of her still couldn't believe that he was her boyfriend. She had always admired him. When he came back, she knew he had changed, but she was able to figure out that fundamentally, he was still the boy she grew up with. But it was still early in their romantic relationship; they needed to learn much about each other, though that would come with time.

Reina then thought about school. She loved her thesis. The topic had always fascinated her, and she enjoyed working on it. The research she was doing would end when she finished her business in Tokyo. After that, it was a matter of writing up her conclusions and preparing her defence. Then, she'd graduate.

Those thoughts then led again towards her mother, her parents. She would have loved her father to be there to see her finish her degree. With how things were turning out and her mother's unresponsiveness, she knew with growing certainty that her mother probably wouldn't be there either.

It was then she remembered her father's words in one of his letters:

一期一会. *Once in a lifetime encounter. Remember this proverb, Rei. Remember to cherish each moment because they only happen once. Always remember to treat everyone with respect and to appreciate each moment you share with them. Our time with people is only temporary, so revere it. Nurture those moments so they become memories that will last a lifetime. I might not be there with you, but know that I will treasure every single moment of your life with you from heaven. Don't worry too much about the details of the future. It is yet to happen. Things always change. People always change. But never forget who you are, your morals and values. Live each moment, my precious daughter.*

CHAPTER 9

Yuuki Maruyama had loved Amai Omoide just as much as he loved his family. He enjoyed seeing the happy faces of his customers. He felt privileged to be a part of other people's celebrations, even if only in a small way. During special occasions, customers shared the sweets they bought from Amai Omoide with the people they loved. He appreciated the more mundane days, though. Time and again, he'd see someone was having a rough day, and he loved watching their eyes light up in appreciation when they saw the confections on display.

Yuuki had always looked up to his older brother, Ichigo. He felt honoured to be able to work with his parents and older brother in keeping the family business going. When Reina was born, he made her a silent promise that he would do his best to keep the business alive for her and future generations.

When he started getting sick, he worried about everything, especially his daughter. After his doctor gave him the grim diagnosis, he decided to carve out a plan that would secure his family and the shop beyond his death.

Before Yuuki had started feeling awry, the owner of the store to the left of Amai Omoide had approached him. The man let him know that he was planning to sell his business. He and his wife had wanted to move back to their hometown of Kobe to be closer to both of their parents. Yuuki had expressed an interest in purchasing the store. At that point, he hadn't told anybody. He had planned to, but his visits to the hospital became more frequent.

The man had reached out to him again, thinking that Yuuki had changed his mind. Yuuki knew the man was in a hurry, so he decided to proceed with the transaction using his own money. He'd titled it under Amai Omoide but with legal paperwork that added his daughter's name once she came of age.

Yuuki loved his wife, Reika, dearly. He had promised a lifetime with her. But he knew that she would not be able to handle his eventual death. He knew that she would make choices that would not be the best but would seem right for her. She had never handled death well. He had seen how her mother's passing had affected her badly. His fate was inevitable, so he made sure there were safeguards in place for Reina. He could only predict so much of his wife's choices, but he was going to make certain that his daughter would have a stable future.

As the days passed, Yuuki realised that he wouldn't be around long enough to start the changes. He wrote detailed instructions in a notebook and asked his brother over when he was home alone.

Ichigo came over one afternoon. "Good afternoon, Yuuki. How are you feeling?"

Smiling at his older brother, he gestured for Ichigo to sit beside him on the tatami cushion. Yuuki then offered Ichigo tea.

"I'm feeling better today, Brother. Thank you for coming."

"Of course, it's no problem at all." Ichigo took a sip of his tea before he continued. "Is there something I can help you with?"

Yuuki nodded as he turned to his side. "I'd like to give you a few things, as well as instructions." He started with his journals. "These are my journals. Please keep them until you believe Rei is ready to have them."

"Wouldn't you want to leave them to Reika instead?" He took the notebooks regardless.

Yuuki shook his head. "Reika, for all her good intentions, would throw these away. She won't want to see anything that will remind her of me. Don't get me wrong. I don't doubt that she loves me and our daughter, but she struggles coping with loss. With her history of postpartum depression…and our recent miscarriage…it is a lot for anybody."

Ichigo froze. "Miscarriage? What?"

Yuuki's face fell with a grief. He cleared his throat before answering his older brother, "When Reika had her annual physical exam, the doctors found that Reika was pregnant." Emotion stated to cloud Yuuki's words as he continued, "When the ultrasound was done, it was an ectopic pregnancy, meaning the baby wasn't growing in Reika's womb. She had to go through emergency surgery. We lost the baby."

Ichigo's jaw dropped. He clasped a hand on his younger brother's shoulder as Yuuki's body started shaking with sobs. Ichigo's heart broke for Yuuki. His brother was born to be a father. He could remember the moment Reina was born. The expression of absolute love was visible in the entirety of Yuuki's being. He would have loved the new baby as much.

After a while, Yuuki calmed enough to continue, "Reika asked me to not tell anyone else for now because she wants time to process and accept, "Because of an ordinance from the Ministry of Health and Welfare, we weren't required to notify the local government about the loss. The baby cannot be added to our family registry. But…Reika and I…she said she felt that it was another daughter. We named her Akari."

Ichigo was stunned. Yuuki's revelation proved to be a secret that weighed heavily on him. Ichigo didn't know how to respond. He didn't know what say. He eventually decided to simply said, "I'm so sorry, brother."

Yuuki offered a sad smile. He took a deep breath to force himself to calm some more. "I'm still trying to think about how to tell Reina. She's so young," he paused before adding, "There is a chance that my death will affect Reika more than even she will realise, especially with this tragedy…our sweet, little Akari. It will be an act of self-preservation on Reika's part to let go of things remind her of me. She'd rather not have anything to remind her of her grief, but Rei is more like me." Running a hand on top of a journal, Yuuki let out a sigh. "She's losing me at a tender age. I'd like for her to have these so that even when I miss her milestones, she will know my love. I'm just grateful that I have time to prepare, especially for her."

Yuuki handed his rother a sports bag followed by several albums, and Ichigo packed them up. Yuuki then produced a wooden box. There was a soft smile on his face as he opened the lid to show his brother what was inside.

"I'm leaving these for Rei as well. I'm sure you'll recognize some of them." Inside were trinkets and collections Yuuki had kept from his childhood. "I'd like to tell you all about them again, for when Rei asks questions I know she'll have." It took a while for Yuuki to share the stories for each piece.

The last thing Yuuki gave his brother was a folder full of documents and a notebook he had prepared for Amai Omoide. Yuuki took the time to explain everything he'd prepared, from finances to the business plan. He also gave his brother all the legal documents they would need.

"Brother." Yuuki made eye contact with Ichigo. "Rei will feel my absence the most. Promise me that you'll be there to help her. I'm not asking you to replace me. Reika, I'm sure, will continue being the best mother she can be for Rei. She might even find it in herself to get married again. I want both of them to find happiness after me. But… please promise me that Rei will be protected no matter what happens after my death."

"That goes without saying, Yuuki. You have my word that Rei will always have my support," Ichigo answered, emotion clogging his throat. He was losing his younger brother. Nothing would make that easier to accept. No preparation would make him feel ready to say goodbye to the man he called Brother. But Ichigo vowed to be strong. The only way he could help his brother was to make sure that Yuuki felt confident he was everything and everyone in good hands, especially his beloved daughter.

Once all was said and done, Yuuki felt completely at peace. A week later, he passed away.

***

It was the anniversary of Yuuki's death. Ichigo still mourned his brother. All of them did. His loss was still felt sharply. Time had passed. Things had changed. There had been some unexpected challenges, but Ichigo had to admit that without Yuuki's foresight, it could have been worse.

Looking at his niece lighting the incense and preparing the flowers in front of Yuuki's grave, Ichigo couldn't help but feel his heart clench in regret that his brother hadn't been given the chance to see his daughter grow up. She'd become an incredible person.

His gaze then went to the young man beside Reina. Ichigo was sure that Yuuki would have given his blessing had he known Hajime Yoshida would become his daughter's unwavering partner.

Hajime and the rest of the Yoshidas had accompanied them that day. It was something he was grateful for. Ichigo and Yuuki had grown up with the Yoshida boys' parents, Issei and Yuuka. Issei and Yuuki had been classmates and best friends, often getting into trouble together. Yuuka had been the third person in their group who tried to keep them out of trouble. More often than not, though, she found herself in the middle of the trouble with the two. It still amused Ichigo that Issei had grown up to be a Shinto priest. But then again, he was aware of the kind soul Issei had. He wouldn't have been his brother's closest friend otherwise. Ichigo had admired his brother's uncanny way of attracting gentle souls; he'd been a good judge of character.

Ichigo felt a hand land on his right shoulder. He looked up and saw it was Issei. "Twelve years. Can you believe it?" Issei commented.

"I know what you mean. There are times when I expect him to turn up at Amai Omoide or at home. It's only when I see Rei that I'm reminded how long it's been," Ichigo answered, glancing again at his niece as she paid her respects to her father.

There was a moment of silence as all those in attendance took a moment to pay their respects and offer prayers.

Issei pushed Ichigo's wheelchair when they started to head back. His wife was walking with the Maruyama matriarch while his eldest's son and his wife walked with Kouji. Following behind them were Reina and his other three sons.

The walk wasn't far to the Yoshida shrine.

"How's rehab going?" Issei asked as the group made their way.

Ichigo sighed. He understood his recovery wouldn't be as fast as he would've like, but it was still frustrating. "I'm told it's going at an ideal pace, but I have to admit, I often wish that it would go faster. When I try to move my left side, though, it reminds me that it's better to do it properly instead of causing more problems."

"Ah! No worries, my friend. I'm sure that you'll be on your feet soon. Just a little more patience," Issei reassured him.

Ichigo chuckled. "I'm glad your son is around to help out and that my parents hired him."

Issei smiled. "I should be the one to thank you and your family, though."

Ichigo looked up in confusion. Issei thought about the last few months, especially the early days after Hajime had returned home. He never said anything, but he knew there was something incredibly difficult his son was dealing with. There was much Hajime hadn't revealed. As a father, Issei felt it in his soul but decided not to pry. His son would approach him if and when he was ready. As the days and weeks passed, Hajime found employment with Amai Omoide and was reacquainted with Reina. After that, Issei saw the changes in Hajime.

"Working at Amai Omoide saved him." Issei refused to say more.

Ichigo thought about what he had been told but didn't ask for more.

CHAPTER 10

Hajime was sluggish. His muscles felt weak. He could feel his head spinning and throbbing. To top it all off, he had a sore throat. It was difficult to swallow. He didn't have to get the thermometer to know he had a very high fever. When he woke up at five in the morning, he had already felt under the weather. He had a brief phone call with Reina before breakfast to let her know that he had received an email from the programmer they contracted to set up the new website for Amai Omoide. After that, he had forced himself to eat a piece of bread and went back to sleep. He was in and out of sleep. When the clock indicated it was noon, he knew he had to figure out his lunch.

He got up to check his refrigerator for something simple to eat. Cooking wasn't an option. He barely had the strength to stand. In his weakened state, cooking would only make him feel worse. Hajime knew it was important for him to eat something before taking medication. At the very least, he had to keep hydrated.

When Hajime realised there weren't any leftovers and that everything else in his fridge required cooking, he closed the door. He willed his frustration away. His brain wasn't working well, to say the least. His jumbled thoughts swirled around as he tried to come up with a solution, but before he could start planning, he heard the doorbell.

Confused as to who it could be, Hajime slowly made his way to the front door. When he opened it, it took him a moment to recover from his surprise when he realised that Reina was standing there.

"Rei, what—"

Reina held up a shopping bag with food, drinks, and medicine. "I didn't like how you sounded on the phone earlier." She walked inside the apartment and closed the door. After toeing her shoes off, she pressed her hand to his forehead. "You're burning up. Have you taken anything yet? Food? Medicine?"

Hajime closed his eyes and allowed himself the comfort of her touch. He was truly grateful but… "You're about have your exams, Rei. I don't want you to catch my cold."

"I'll be fine," was her simple response as she gave him a reassuring smile. "Now, do you want to get to bed or lounge in the living room while I prepare you something?"

Too sick to argue, Hajime resigned himself to accepting her help. "I think I'd like to lie down. I have a headache."

A look of concern crossed her features. She followed him to his room and tucked him in. Once she could see that he was comfortable, Reina stuck a cooling patch on his forehead. "Are you hungry?"

"Yes and no. I don't have much of an appetite, but I know I have to eat something. I haven't had anything but a piece of toast from this morning."

That's hardly anything, Reina thought to herself. "All right then. Why don't you try to rest a bit while I prepare something for you?"

Hajime nodded and closed his eyes. He didn't know how much time had passed or that he'd fallen asleep. The next thing he knew, he opened his eyes and saw the wall clock. It was a quarter past two.

He looked to his right and saw Reina studying at his desk. When he moved to face her, it caught her attention. She looked up and rolled the chair closer to the bed.

"How are you feeling?" she asked.

"My headache is a bit better. It isn't pounding as much as earlier."

Reina nodded. "That's good." She then handed him an insulated mug. "Here. Try this ginger tea I've prepared. Do you think you'll be up for some porridge?"

Hajime took a sip and got up from bed. "I'll follow you to the kitchen."

After a quick trip to the bathroom, Hajime sat at the table. Reina had been prepared and offered him a bowl of rice porridge. Hajime brought his hand together and offered his thanks for the food with a quick, "Itadakimasu."

"Meshiagare," Reina returned his courtesy as she sat down in front of him with her own cup of tea.

A comfortable silence settled between the two as Hajime slowly finished the meal Reina prepared for him.

"Gochisousamadeshita." He clapped his hands together again after eating, expressing his thanks.

"Would you like more tea?" Reina asked as she took the bowl and placed it on the sink.

"Yes, please." Hajime liked the taste of the ginger tea his girlfriend prepared. There was a certain warmth to it, not to mention that it made his throat feel a lot better. He could taste a hint of cloves. Knowing her, she would have added honey too.

Reina went inside his room to get the thermometer and his medicine. "Thank you," he called after her.

"You're welcome."

"I've been noticing this for a while now, Rei. You have an affinity with tea—an intuitive sense for making the perfect kind to complement any food. Haruka couldn't stop talking about the special tea mixture you gave her for her birthday. She's savouring it as much as possible."

Reina blushed. "I can't really take all the credit. Tea was a father-daughter thing. Dad loved tea. He'd bring me to enjoy the traditional tea ceremony often. On his days off, we would experiment together about the different tea combinations. Mom liked baking so she would say, my dad and I were in charge of tea while she made something. Almost every Sunday, my parents would take me to different tea shops and cafes to try out things we've never tried before. The following weekend, we would try to re-create the tastes. That all stopped when my dad got sick. He became too sick to go out often. When I started living on my own, I picked up the habit again."

Hajime was pleasantly surprised. He never witnessed that side of Reina and her parents while he was growing up. He could understand why she'd taken up the habit again. He was proud of her for doing so.

"Would you be open to experimenting with desserts with me? I'll cook and you'll figure out the tea?" His voice was soft.

It brought a smile to Reina's face. She never imagined to be sharing one of her hobbies with another person again. "I'd really, really like that."

The two shared a sweet moment before Hajime commented, "One day, I'd like for you to meet my closest friends in France." There was a fondness in his gaze when he remembered his three closest French friends. Sharing the kitchen and practicing recipes brought a lot of memories he shared with Felipe, whom Hajime went to culinary school with. The two of them would practice their culinary skills and often had their other two roommates, twin brothers – Alexandre and Raphael – as taste testers. They weathered some interesting challenges together, and they'd become like family. Sometime in the future, Hajime would like to introduce Reina to them.

"I would love that," Reina replied with smile of her own. "Is it okay for me to ask you about France?"

"You can ask me anything, Rei,"

Reina blushed again. "I know...it's just..."

Hajime stood. He gently took her hands and pulled her with him towards the sofa. He sat down and took her in his arms. With her head resting on his collarbone, Hajime said, "I have a feeling I know what you want to ask about if you are this tongue-tied. I want you to know, I don't talk about it because it still makes me angry. I had never truly felt ready to talk about it – raw and no holding back."

Reina took a moment to meet his gaze. "Have you...tried talking about it with other people?" she asked carefully as she tried to sit up, but his arms prevented her from going far.

Hajime smiled. He softly brushed the side of her face with the backs of his fingers. "I have. But not outside counselling sessions. I haven't felt ready to talk about the whole truth with other people but I feel ready now. I want to tell you. I won't hide it from you—not ever."

He watched her eyes soften. He had mentioned to Reina at one time about his counselling sessions. He hadn't intimated details, only that he thought he needed it. She supported him and reassured him that she would wait for him when he was ready to explain everything. It seemed that it was in that moment. Still, she wanted him to be sure and not feel pressured. "Hajime," she started, "You should know I'll never force you. Encourage you, maybe but never force. If you'd like to talk about it, I'll listen."

Hajime pulled her against his chest and tightened his embrace. He laid a kiss on her forehead and encouraged her to settle against him. "Get comfortable because it's a long and complicated story. It started last December, seven months before I returned to Japan."

CHAPTER 11

December 27th (seven months before Hajime returned to Japan)

It was past midnight. It had been another busy day at the restaurant and Hajime was accompanying Emily Lefebvre, the owner of the restaurant, close for the day. It had become a normal routine for Hajime to stay with the old lady as Emily made sure everything was settled for the night. It had started when Hajime got delayed one evening because of the preparations he had to do for the breads and cakes of the next day. There had been a lot of orders for la Fête de Nationale – Bastille Day. Celebrated every July 14th, France's National Day was an important holiday to commemorate the pivotal moment of the French Revolution.

Hajime noticed his delay meant that the owner was also delayed in her nightly routine. Riddled with guilt, Hajime asked if he could help with anything. Emily was quick to pacify the young man and told him to go home. It didn't feel right for Hajime to leave the elderly woman by herself especially knowing that Emily had a heart condition and noticed that it was nearing one in the morning. Hajime had patiently waited outside, which surprised Emily after she secured the final locks. Hajime had walked the older lady to her car and excused himself to go home.

After that first night, Hajime got curious if it were the same every day. He was uncomfortable knowing that Emily's nightly routine left her somewhat vulnerable in the wee hours of the morning. He decided to observe for the next few days and had come to the realisation that on average, the widow left for home a few minutes after midnight. It wasn't a difficult decision to stay to make sure Emily was safe every night. It was the least he could do for the older woman Hajime had come to admire and respect.

Night after night, Hajime would wait for Emily outside to walk her to her car. It was a start of a close friendship between Emily and Hajime. The older woman started sharing stories with Hajime about how she and her husband, Arnaud, had started the restaurant. She had also intimated that she and Arnaud had wanted to have children but after three miscarriages, they accepted that fact that they would remain childless and poured everything they had into the restaurant. The elderly woman then started allowing Hajime to help her do the double checking around the kitchen, the front of the store, and the inventory while she finished checking the financial documents, reservations, and other files. It allowed her to leave for home earlier.

"Hajime," Emily called him to her office. She leaned back on her office chair and waited to the young man to sit. They both had finished double checking everything and were ready to leave. But Emily decided that it was the perfect time to share with the man what she had been contemplating for several months, "I'm tired." Hajime kept quiet. "I have thought about this for a while now. With Arnaud gone, I want to return to my hometown. I want to open a small bakery. I was hoping you are open to being my head pâtissier. I've already talked with Felipe and he is willing to be my head baker. What do you think?"

It had taken Hajime by surprise. He didn't expect Emily to say that. Emily gave a short laugh at the surprise clearly shown on the face of her young friend, "It's December 27th. I'm sure you'll want to think this through. I won't be pursuing this plan until next month. I thought I'd give you my offer so you have enough time to consider your options. I am still having my lawyer draw new contracts as well as fixing other major details of the new shop and preparing for the new management of this one. I expect you and Felipe to truly consider what you want and give me an answer before February of next year."

***

December 31st (seven months before Hajime returned to Japan)

In the late afternoon, Alexandre, Hajime, and Felipe were scrambling to finish all the preparations they needed to for their New Year's celebration. They originally planned to have a party but with how busy all of them got after Christmas, the roommates decided to have a simple, quiet celebration instead.

Their plans shifted again when Raphael said that he had to work over the New Year. Raphael was on-duty at the fire station until the second of January since he took the Christmas holiday off. Alexandre suggested dropping by to wish his twin and the rest of the firemen on duty a Happy New Year before he, Felipe and Hajime headed to Felipe's parents' house.

The Martinez family pretty much adopted Hajime and the twins during the first year they had become their eldest son, Felipe's roommates. There had been a lot of weekends where Felipe's mom, Martina, would invite all of them for Sunday, family lunch. During exam season, Martina would drop off dinner to make sure all four men had a decent meal while studying. It had become a standing tradition that New Year's Day would be spent at the Martinez' house.

"Has Emily talked with you yet, Hajime?" Felipe asked as he was placing the tray of pie into the oven. It was decided that since Raphael was going to miss the annual New Year's Day celebration of the Martinez family, the three men were going to bring food to the fire station. The paella's ingredients were ready on different containers in the refrigerator. Felipe was going to be cooking in the morning. The blueberry pie was the last of the food items they planned on dropping off.

"Yes, she has. I'm still considering it. It is a good opportunity but at the same time, my mom has been more and more vocal about wanting me back in Japan." Hajime answered. He was standing in front of the sink, doing the dishes.

Before anyone could comment, a knock from the front door sounded. All three men looked at each other. They weren't expecting anyone.

Alexandre went to check while the other two continued their tasks around the kitchen.

"Hajime, darling," came the voice of Hajime's girlfriend, Juliette. She walked towards her boyfriend and kissed him in the cheek. Hajime was surprised to see her after she had been adamant in telling him she wasn't going to be in Paris for the New Year. She and her friends were going on an all-girls trip she said.

Alexandre noticed though that both Felipe AND Hajime froze from the sound of the woman's voice. He never liked Juliette but tolerated her because of Hajime. There was something about the woman that had his guards up. Alexandre knew that his brother and Felipe felt the same. No one said anything regarding their perceptions in respect to their friend. Lately, Alexandre had observed a subtle change in Hajime, especially when the subject of Juliette came up. He couldn't put his finger on it but Alexandre had a feeling the relationship between his friend and Juliette would be ending soon.

***

January 1st (six months before Hajime returned to Japan)

Hajime left his room and ran a hand down in face in frustration. It was past one in the morning. His two roommates were still in the living room having a quiet conversation. Hajime flopped down beside Felipe on the couch.

"How are you holding up, my friend?" Felipe asked as he offered beer to Hajime.

Hajime declined the offer before answering, "I don't know what's going on with Juliette anymore. She started taking her clothes off when I helped her to my room and pulled the covers for her. I tried to stop her but...it's a good thing she's too drunk and passed out quickly or it would have been very ugly."

"All that in a few minutes? You barely escorted her to your room five minutes ago." Alexandre commented.

Hajime sighed. "She's turning out to be a completely different person than from what I thought. I think she's having an affair. There's this wall...I can't really explain it."

Felipe and Alexandre exchanged glances. Neither said anything. There was a comfortable silence shared by the three. It was only broken when Hajime's phone chimed to alert him to a message.

Hajime stood and headed to the balcony. He immediately called home.

While Hajime was in a call with his family in Japan, Alexandre and Felipe started talking again.

"If Juliette's behaviour tonight doesn't force Hajime to break up with her, I'm not sure what will." Alexandre commented.

Felipe nodded and took a swig of beer. "They lasted longer than I expected. Three months is still three months."

Alexandre snorted. "You talk as if it's a given they're separating."

"Like you're not sure either," Felipe responded. "You can't tell me that you didn't notice how withdrawn Hajime became the more the night progressed. He's more polite than actually making an effort as a boyfriend."

Hajime walked towards the living room and told his roommates, "My family wants to greet you a Happy New Year."

Felipe and Alexandre sat up and smiled. Hajime adjusted his phone to capture the three of them.

***

February 23rd (six months before Hajime returned to Japan)

It had been a trying month. For some reason, Pierre had been especially short with him since after the New Year. Hajime understood that the man was the executive chef and it was his responsibility that everything in the kitchen worked as they should. It was the little things at first – Hajime's desserts didn't look the same; not instructing the junior chef Hajime was paired with correctly; not filling out the order requests for ingredients on time; and, time management issues.

Hajime had more reprimands from January to that day than he had ever since he started working at the restaurant four years prior. He wasn't the only one who noticed. Every single one of his co-workers had approached him to ask what was wrong. They had always been a cohesive team and problems didn't escalate into bigger ones because there would always be someone to help. It was obvious that Hajime was being singled out and it all started a few days after the New Year when the new executive chef took over kitchen management – Pierre Lefebvre. With Emily taken ill, all management responsibilities fell to Pierre.

"This is getting ridiculous," Felipe commented as turned off the burner. Pierre had called Hajime out while they were finishing their prep work before the dinner service in three hours. The other chefs exchanged looks with one another.

It didn't take long before Pierre re-entered the kitchen. His demeanour didn't reveal anything but professionalism. It got everyone wondering what was going on since Hajime failed to return

"Stephen," Pierre called out to the junior chef helping with the dessert station with Hajime. The said man stepped forward and Pierre continued, "As you all know, my aunt Emily will be opening a shop in our hometown while I take over this restaurant. Stephen, you will be given the position of head pâtissier. Now, let's all get back to work. Dinner service will be in a few hours." The announcement left every one of them stunned. They knew that Emily had offered the job to Hajime. Stephen was to take over Hajime's position once he left.

"Hold on," Felipe immediately asked. "Emily offered that position to Hajime,"

Pierre coldly looked back and cut Felipe off, "My aunt is too sick at the moment to make any kind of decision related to the restaurant and the new shop. I have her power of attorney to make these decisions. If you must know, Hajime has been laid off," This brought shock and murmurs of disbelief to erupt around the kitchen. "It has been found out that he has been abusing his close relationship with my aunt to embezzling money." This accusation brought more reactions of disbelief.

"You're lying! Hajime would never do that!" Felipe's impassioned defence on his friend. There were several agreements that sounded from their different colleagues.

"Well, as much as I didn't want to believe it too, upon review of the ledgers, there had been number discrepancies found. Further investigation was done and it was traced that a lot of those transactions were doctored after hours. Aside from my aunt, the only person who was here with her is Hajime. It is the only logical explanation."

"That's complete and utter bull," Felipe took off his apron and started walking out of the kitchen.

"If you walk out that door, you don't have a job here anymore too," Pierre threatened.

"See if I care! I will not work in a place that gives accusations that could destroy a man's reputation – not to mention his life!" Felipe walked out without a glance back. He was hurling out some choice Spanish curses and his whole body radiated anger. What he didn't know is that almost every single one of the chefs he and Hajime had worked with for the past four years had also walked out, leaving only two junior chefs.

Hajime arrived at the apartment he shared with two roommates. They'd been living together since he'd moved to France.

Raphael was sitting in front of the TV watching the news. He seemed to have the day off from work. He turned towards the door and said as soon as he saw Hajime, "You're early. What's up?"

Before Hajime could answer. The door shot open again, and their other roommate, Felipe, angrily entered. He was yelling expletives.

Raphael turned off the TV and stood up. He was in the process of asking what had happened with both his roommates when a knock sounded at the door.

Hajime opened it and was stunned when he saw two uniformed officers there. He froze when he realised they were there to arrest him, but he didn't fight back as they cuffed him.

Felipe loudly protested, prompting one officer to hold him back. Hajime could honestly say that his mind was blank; he didn't understand what was being said.

In the background, Raphael was on the phone with his brother, Alexandre, a lawyer. Raphael exchanged a worried glance with Felipe.

As the police led Hajime out, Felipe yelled, "Don't worry, Hajime. We will get you out. You are innocent! Don't you forget that!"

***

"It took a day before Alexandre could get me out. With regards to the embezzling issue, Alexandre tells me that it is still an active investigation. From what I understand, the police are still investigating Pierre and Juliette – what their roles are since they both have the title of executive chef and accountant respectively. It is being hypothesized that Pierre targeted me as a scapegoat because I had a relationship with Juliette. It doesn't take that much effort to work out that they are involved. I have learned not to care. Alexandre also sued them on my behalf for defamation of character and illegal dismissal. It was a quick case because Pierre offered no contest. All of it was settled outside of court. The settlement money has been processed and deposited by Alexandre to my French bank account. I feel bad for Emily, though, because I know how she and her husband had put their entire lives into the restaurant. The silver lining to all of it is that she's no longer around to witness this unfolding. I regret not being able to say goodbye to her." Hajime said as he ran a hand through Reina's hair.

"I'm glad Alexandre was able to get you out." Reina's voice was soft. "I don't know much about the law, especially French law, but I'm supposing it wasn't easy given it took about a day to get you out," she commented.

Hajime was silent. This was the part that no one aside from him and Alexandre knew – and the counsellor he reached out to via teletherapy recently. It was the main thing that made him closed off and reluctant to talk about things with others. Reina noticed the slight change in Hajime's countenance. She started to sit up but Hajime's arms tightened around her, stopping all movement.

Hajime cleared his throat and forced the words out of his mouth. "There are a lot of depraved people in the world. It was… unfortunately…that I was locked up with some of them," Hajime's heart started beating faster at his distress. He couldn't keep his emotions out of his voice. "I was attacked, Reina," Hajime's voice broke just as Reina gasped in shock. She could feel tears pooling at the corner of her eyes. She unconsciously tightened her grip on Hajime's shirt. "The attack was…emasculating…I was angry about everything. I felt this immense guilt that I wasn't strong enough to fight back. For a long time, I felt like it was my fault…all of it. There was so much anger that I learned to internalise it…to keep in a tightly contained box inside…pretend I was fine so that I don't accidentally lash out. But, through counselling I realised it only made me detached and somewhat cold. Coming home to Japan… it saved my life, Reina, not only because I am surrounded by people who love me but…especially re-establishing a relationship with you… it made me realise I didn't lose who I truly was before all the nastiness happened. It pushed me to ask for help."

With that admission, Reina buried her face against Hajime's chest, her arms clinched tightly around him with her fingers fisting the back of his shirt. Silent tears fell from her eyes.

Hajime rested his chin atop her head. He could feel his shirt dampen with Reina's tears. "Shh…"

"Why are you the one reassuring me when, it's you…," she answered, burrowing against him further.

He let out an amused laugh. To be quite honest, Hajime didn't know where the laughter came from. It was such a serious issue but after having lived in the darkness alone for such a long time, opening to Reina about one of his darkest times was more of a relief than anything. He wasn't alone. He had this wonderful woman in his arms. A part of him felt guilty of bringing Reina into his darkness but the words of his counsellor came back to him, "It isn't you bringing another person into the darkness. It is you breaking free of the darkness and sharing the light with the person you've chosen to open to. You are allowing the light into that dark hour and slowly silencing it until nothing is hidden in the shadows…shadows that wait for the perfect moment to attack you."

"Hey! Don't laugh!" Reina sat up and looked at Hajime. He could see in her eyes that she was genuinely upset for him. "I don't even know what to say, Hajime. The false accusation…the attack," Tears further fell from her eyes. Hajime gently wiped them away. "You didn't deserve any of it!"

Hajime didn't say or react for a moment. He quietly looked at the woman he was steadily falling deeper and deeper in love with.

Reaching up to cup his face, Reina closed her eyes and leaned her forehead against his. "I know it must have taken you such a great deal of strength to reveal something as horrible as that. Your trust in me…I will treasure it. I don't know the right words to say… you'll have to help me, love. I wish I could make it all go away…that it never happened…but…I'm right here, Hajime. You are not alone anymore. Also…I am in awe of you. To have the courage to ask for help…for telling me now…you simply amaze me. You are NOT a victim. You are a survivor. Your strength simply is magnificent."

Her love made his heart beat for a whole different reason. The warmth that spread through him was pushing away the coldness that usually accompanied the horrid memory. Unbeknownst to him, Hajime had silent tears falling down his eyes as well. Reina kissed them away before hugging him to her.

"It took me a while, but my mind finally caught up in realising that I am home. I suppose I had to approach the whole recovery process that was right for me. I had to be the one to say, 'I need help.' And I am…getting help. I had to truly believe first that there is strength in admitting I need help…that even as a man, acknowledging I'm at a loss is not bad. I've been having teletherapy with a professional for almost two months now. I've accepted that it did happen and there isn't anything that could be done to undo it. I survived it. One of my roommates—Alexandre's twin, Raphael, told me once that we are our choices. I am responsible for my actions, big or small. That includes how I am choosing to react. My counsellor helped me forgive myself in terms of feeling guilty of not being strong enough to stop it and for allowing myself to close myself off. It's still a struggle to be completely at peace but time will help…and so does keeping with my counselling sessions…my family…you. So… no more tears, my little love. Don't waste your anger on something in the past. Regardless of what happened…it brought me home."

The two enjoyed a peaceful silence. It allowed them to process what had been shared and what had just happened.

It made Reina think of dark secrets of her own. "Hajime…" She started softly. "I want to share something no one aside from my family and your parents know."

CHAPTER 12

1863, Third year of Bunkyuu, Edo Period

Shiori was sweeping the street just outside their shop entrance in the middle of the afternoon. It was a very hot summer day, and she thought of sprinkling water to make it a little cooler. Her two sons were inside with their father.

A sigh left her lips. Shiori was grateful that her sons were healthy, and business was slowly picking up but the tension around Kyoto was concerning. Aside from insurgents roaming the streets, samurai belonging to different domains were usually at contention with each other. There were stores and business that are claimed by a domain, which meant the absolute protection from their benefactors but disdain from rival domains. It was common to see some clashes along the streets, especially in highly popular areas where chances of meeting a samurai from another domain was high.

While Amai Omoide wasn't situation in the heart of Kyoto, their area still saw their fair share of violence. Riku and Shiori kept their heads down and worked.

As Shiori was about to enter, something fell behind her, and she turned, then gasped at what she saw.

Two bloody samurai. One dropped to the street while the other, clearly injured, tried to help his comrade.

The samurai who was barely standing heard Shiori's gasp. His countenance immediately turned defensive, softening a little when he realised that he was facing a woman – a civilian.

Shiori was shaking, but somehow found the courage to speak, she said, "My Lord, I have two small babies inside with my husband. We are simple folks. Please…we don't wish you harm." The man remained silent, his eyes still indifferent. Shiori gulped. She had never talked with a samurai before. It was usually her father or her husband who talked directly to them when the samurai passed through Shiori's hometown. She added, "May I offer assistance? My father was a doctor in our village. I might not know much, but I can at least offer some help to you and your friend."

She was able to see a slight change in the man's eyes. He looked down at his friend. If he didn't get help soon, he would die right there in the street. His own strength was dwindling.

"Please," came his simple reply.

Shiori gave a nod. "Let me help you." Without waiting for another reply, Shiori stepped beside the fallen man. "There have been a lot of insurgents wandering here lately. We have to get you both inside quickly. Unfortunately, there isn't a lot of help available in this part of Kyoto."

The man knew she spoke the truth. He and his partner were samurai for the Satsuma. The Satsuma had been hearing a lot of insurgent activity around Kyoto. The man and his comrade weren't tasked to deal with the insurgents but rather, gather intel around the capital, especially regarding the behaviour and actions of the samurais from the other domains. But they had been careless. They had a nasty encounter with a few Choshu samurai. While they were successful in eliminating all their opponents, they were severely injured. His friend would surely have died if fate decided to intervene, and they were able to cross paths with the woman currently helping them.

Riku was stunned when his wife staggered into their house with some injured samurai. He snapped out of his trance when his wife urgently said, "Riku, there is a lot of blood outside. Try to wash it away with water as much as you can. Then help me, please."

As her husband did as she asked, she asked the more conscious samurai, "Ronin pass through here around this time of day. That's why all of us with stores close early."

As they settled in the backroom, Shiori's three-year-old son Kouki looked up and called for his mother, his child's gaze brimming with curiosity.

"Kouki, take care of your brother. Mother and Father are just helping these gentlemen. But before that, can you get all the linens on the shelf for me?"

Small feet eagerly pattered on the floor. Kouki was eager to do his mother's bidding; he liked helping his parents. Now that he was a big brother, they'd said, he could help. He was taught that the bigger he got, the more responsibilities he was expected to fulfil.

"You have a smart boy," the samurai commented.

"Thank you, My Lord. He has been through a lot in his young life. I suppose life is being a good teacher to him."

Shiori then turned her attention to the unconscious man in front of her. As the only child of the village healer in the village, Shiori had helped her father a lot. Even after she and Riku had gotten married, her father would often send for her to assist for a few hours. While it wasn't usual practice in their time, her father didn't have a choice since all her sisters had moved out of the village with their husbands. Her parents had no sons, but four daughters. He loved them all and treated them well, but no one was left to take over his practice. His apprentice had gone to Edo to learn more with his teacher's blessing. Yet all that didn't matter anymore as the village had been destroyed.

"Riku, could you get me my sewing kit? We need to stop this bleeding."

It was a tense few hours. In between, Riku excused himself to prepare a simple meal for his family and guests.

"I don't have all the things needed here but rest assured, My Lord. Having cleaned both your wounds and closed some of his bigger ones, it looks like it isn't as bad as we all thought. When you get wherever you need to be, both of you should be looked at by a real doctor to make sure," Shiori suggested as she wiped her hands.

She looked over at the other futon and smiled when she saw both her sons fast asleep. Tomorrow would be another day, but for now, they were alive. They had done their best to help complete strangers. Whether it would bring them blessings or death, Shiori couldn't find it in herself to worry. She hoped that her sons would help people without expecting anything in return. It was something her father had passed on to her—to help everyone in need whether there'd be any thanks in return.

It was one reason why she had always loved being married into the Maruyama clan. While they were talented artisans, they worked to make people smile with their sweets. It was common for the Maruyamas to feed their hungry neighbours whenever the family had extras. Her father had been at ease leaving her in the hands of the Maruyama family.

"Mrs. Maruyama"—the samurai bowed in extreme gratitude—"I will be heading back this evening to let my superiors know that we are alive. I will return tomorrow with help to get my comrade back home. I apologise for the inconvenience." He bowed again.

"Oh, please, My Lord" Shiori was quick to assuage, "it is an honour to help samurai in need." She bowed low with humility.

"My wife is right, My Lord." Riku also bowed. "We might not have much, but we'd like to believe there are still a lot of good in the world. We are honoured to be of service."

The samurai bowed again as he took his swords and stood. "I am from the Satsuma domain. Your selfless actions will not be forgotten. Thank you for treating us and for offering food. Please excuse me."

Based on experience, it was very rare that samurai would be completely cordial or accept help from peasants. The samurai's warrior code, bushido, prevented them from asking for help. But, for the past months, Riku and Shiori had only really come across and interacted with ronin. Perhaps they acted differently if they still served a master. Whatever happened that day, all those involved believed it was fate.

True to his word, the Satsuma samurai came back early the next day with a few more samurai. Their comrade had woken up before dawn, and the Maruyama couple explained what had happened. Riku helped the man do his business while Shiori prepared him a simple meal with the rest of her family.

Just before they left, another Satsuma samurai said, "I am the unit leader of the men you've helped. Thank you for tending to their wounds and feeding them. In return, know that your deeds have reached the leaders of Satsuma. You need not worry. As of today, you are under Satsuma protection. As we are in Kyoto, you are free to conduct business as normal, regardless of clientele. But where safety is concerned, the Satsuma will take charge. You will no longer need to worry about the insurgents coming through this area."

The Maruyama couple couldn't help bowing in gratitude several times. Tears formed in Shiori's eyes. As a mother, knowing that she wouldn't have to constantly worry about her sons growing up in a lawless environment had come with much welcome.

What the Maruyama couple didn't realise was that the Satsuma protection would be a boon to their family for generations to come.

***

"What do you mean?" Hajime asked.

Reina took a deep breath before she sat back against the sofa. She closed her eyes. It was something she never talked about, not even with Aika. The words always got stuck in her throat. At that moment, she wanted Hajime to know.

She wasn't lying when she admitted she was falling in love with Hajime. After hearing his story, unembellished and raw, she felt reassured that she too could share something painful without judgment.

Hajime, unknowingly, gave her the courage to speak about one of the dark periods of her life. It felt right that Hajime would be the first person to hear about all the details from her.

"When I came back to live here in Kyoto, what did your mom tell you?" Reina asked.

"Only that you had moved back and would be living with your uncle and grandparents."

Reina nodded. She took Hajime's hand in her own, hoping the simple act would embolden her.

***

It was April. Reina was starting her last year of junior high school. She returned home late because her club activities ran late. But if she were really honest with herself, she dreaded coming home.

It was a very cold home. She couldn't help but miss her previous home in Kyoto. She felt like a stranger in her mother's new home here in Tokyo. Her stepfather barely talked to or even acknowledged her. When he did, he always treated her coldly, even in her mother's presence. There had been a few times where she was slapped by her stepfather for the simplest of transgressions like forgetting to take out the trash, bought the wrong condiment at the store, or, simply not answering his question as fast as he would like. Hitting her was far in between since most of the time, he acted as if she didn't exist and with her mother not saying anything, Reina decided to let it go.

When Reina first met her then to-be-stepfather, she hadn't felt comfortable and thought the man was far from loving before her mother married Yuito Suzuki. The one time Reina voiced her concerns while her mother and Yuito were still dating, her mother reacted badly. For some reason, it felt like Reika hated her only daughter; Reina noticed that her mother would hardly look at her unless it was absolutely necessary.

The temptation to tell her uncle Ichigo about the situation grew more enticing every time he called. Her promise to her father on his deathbed stopped her. During his last moments, Reina had been by his side at the hospital. Her mother had been absent. Her father explained that her mother didn't do well with death and implored her not to hate her mother for her absence. He made her promise that no matter what happened in the future and when he was no longer around, Reina would always love her mother.

Reina could still remember holding her father's hand. She had been crying because she had seen how weak he had gotten so quickly. They were enjoying tea in the living room after she had gotten home from school when her father suddenly collapsed. Her mother wasn't home, Reina could remember panicking. She called for emergency services using her father's phone all the while staying by her father's side.

At the hospital, things were a blur. The nurse asked her to wait in the waiting room while they attended to her dad. While waiting, Reina had the presence of mind to call her mother and the rest of her family. She didn't wait long before her uncle and grandparents arrived. Her mother was the last to arrive.

Reina wasn't sure how much time elapsed before a doctor approached them. As a child, she didn't understand the jargon the doctor was explaining. The only thing she understood was her father was in critical condition and it wasn't expected that he would be getting better. Any memories from that point were fuzzy because the next clear memory Reina had was staying at her father's bedside, holding his hand.

Yuuki roused and slowly realised that there was a small hand tightly gripping his hard. He turned and saw his daughter's head on top of their clasped hands, crying. He slowly reached out with his free hand and patted Reina on the head. Yuuki smiled when his daughter automatically sat up. His heart clenched when he saw Reina's face crumble. Her expression was a mix of relief and despair.

"There, there, Rei," Yuuki squeezed her hand. He didn't have the strength to reach out to her again. "Everything is going to be all right."

"Daddy, please don't leave me! The doctor said...the doctor said..." Reina couldn't contain her tears.

Yuuki's heart broke. With the little energy he had, he moved and made space for his daughter on the bed. "Come here, Rei," His eight-year-old daughter tucked herself against his side, tightly wrapping her arms around her father as best as she could. "I'm not leaving you, Rei. You might not see me anymore but I'm still right here," he pointed to her head, "and most especially here," he then pointed to her heart. He then squeezed Reina closer and laid a kiss on her forehead, silent tears falling from his eyes. Oh, how he wished things were different. He would never see his daughter graduate, fall in love, get married, have kids, and more.

Yuuki looked around the room. There was no one else there aside from him and his daughter. He noticed his wife wasn't around. He let out a tired sigh. He had expected it. She didn't do well with death.

"Rei," he waited for his daughter to look up. Yuuki wiped her tears and said, "where are your mother, uncle and grandparents?"

"Uncle Ichigo went to check the store. They left in such a hurry that Mrs. Ito had to close. He wanted to make sure everything was okay and said he would be back before dinner. Grandpa and Grandma just left to buy food not too long ago. Mom..." Reina's voice trailed off as she looked down. "She said she was going back to work to finish some documents. She didn't say when she'd be back."

Yuuki could see the confusion and disappointment on Reina's face when she told him about her mother. "Rei, look at me," he made sure they had eye contact. "I know you can't understand why your mother isn't here right now. Your grandmother was the only parent she ever knew growing up and when she died, your mom had a terrible time. She doesn't do well in dealing with death. She will try to deny bad things are happening. When I'm gone, she will not like to look at things that will remind her of me. Do not hate her for that. That is the only way she knows how to cope with loss...to survive. You might not understand fully...or see it...but deep down she loves you...and me."

Reina could feel her eyes filling with tears again as soon as her father mentioned the future after he had gone "I don't want to lose you, daddy, *please stay!"* She wrapped her arms around Yuuki with as much strength as she could.

Yuuki hugged his beloved daughter as much as his feeble arms could. "I love you, Reina, never, ever forget that."

"I love you too, daddy."

"You'll be a good girl for me, right?" On Reina's nod, "Promise me that you'll listen to mommy...no matter what happens...no matter how mommy seems to change...you'll love her enough for you and me. Promise me that you'll always remember that you are my strong and brave little girl. Can you promise that, Rei?" Another nod. "You'll also always have Uncle Ichigo and your grandparents. Mr. And Mrs. Yoshida. Your friends, the Yoshida brothers. You'll be never alone, my love. Never forget that mommy loves you...I love you and I'll always be with you."

No other words were spoken as father and daughter fell asleep holding each other...only...the father never woke up.

It was becoming more and more difficult to live up to the promise, but Reina gave her word on her father's deathbed. More than anything, she loved her father very much.

"I'm home," she called out as soon as she entered the house, then sighed when there was no response. This was a usual occurrence recently. She removed her shoes and started for the stairs. The lights were turned on all over the house, so she knew her mother or Yuito was home.

Reina gathered her bags before heading upstairs to her room to change out of her uniform before looking for her mother. If Reika wasn't there, Reina would wait for her mother in her room. She wanted to stay as clear as possible from Yuito.

While he wasn't mostly violent anymore, he had more negative energy about him that made her uncomfortable, especially as of late. From what she gathered, he was having some problems at his office. She would often hear him complaining to Reika, while her mom never said anything. Reina worried he'd take it out on the wrong person one day. Having experienced being slapped several times, Reina knew that the somewhat tenuous control Yuito had on his anger would eventually snap. She didn't *want to be on the receiving end of that as much as she didn't wish her mother to be hurt.*

Reina knew that her mother could intentionally turn a blind eye towards a lot of things regarding her husband in order to keep him – to keep the happiness that she craved after her father's death. Reina was aware about her mother's preferences from the moment she had been screamed for raising concerns about Yuito before her mother married the man. Through the years she had seen how her mother would try to appease the man.

As she was ascending the stairs, Reina heard yelling. She stopped and tried to process what was going on. It seemed that Yuito was shouting at someone, but based on what he was saying, it didn't seem like he was shouting at her mother. Reina decided to hurry to her room, but just as she reached the landing of the second floor, Yuito stormed out of the master bedroom. He in a rampage, holding his phone to his ear. He didn't see her as he was blinded by rage.

Reina wasn't sure what happened. She felt only the sensation of falling before everything went dark.

Her next conscious thought was riddled with confusion. She wasn't sure where she was, but then her Uncle Ichigo's face came into view. His face registered with a mixture of relief and concern, but Reina couldn't really process what'd happened.

"Uncle? What—" Reina started, but then she heard her mother's voice.

"Ah, good, you are awake."

Reina turned towards the door. Her confusion mounted. Her mother was carrying her school bag, her sports bag, and a huge piece of luggage. Her expression was stoic, her voice void of emotion.

"Here are your things. You will be living with your uncle. He's taking you back to Kyoto. I'm sorry I am not capable of being the mother you need," her mother's voice started breaking as she finished her spiel, betraying the gravity of pain Reika was hoping not to show her daughter.

With little preamble, not even giving time for Reina to react or say anything, Reika walked out of her daughter's life.

Reina turned her panicked gaze to her uncle. Ichigo's heart broke for his niece.

"Rei," he started slowly, "you fell down the stairs. Your left arm's broken, and you've injured your ribs. You also hit your head, so you have a mild concussion."

"'Uncle…'" *Tears welled in her eyes. The reality of what was going on was catching up.*

"There aren't any words that will make all this go away or make you feel better. But…Rei, I am taking you home." *Patting his niece's uninjured hand and choking on some of his words, he said,* "You will get through this. You have me, your grandparents, and your friends in Kyoto. It's hard to understand right now but, Rei, your family loves you."

***

Reina took a strengthening breath, hoping to control her emotions. "Your mom…" Some tears escaped her eyes, and she was quick to wipe them away. "Your parents…Uncle Ichigo told them what happened. It was difficult not to since they found out about my return when they saw me at Amai Omoide, trying to do work on assignments from my new school. I had a cast on, and the doctors here hadn't given me clearance to return to school physically. They all decided, my uncle and grandparents, to let them know since they are my father's best friends, and I have always been close to your family. Family is what I needed…to be surrounded by people who love me as I slowly recovered. But they collectively decided to keep the details to themselves to help me heal."

Reina looked into Hajime's eyes and gave a small smile. "Everybody opened their arms and welcomed me back. Your mom… she gave me a mother's hug." More tears fell from her eyes as she remembered what it felt like to experience a mother's love again.

Hajime couldn't help it anymore and pulled her towards him. He wrapped an arm around her waist, and the other cupped the back of her head. He stayed silent, giving her space to finish saying what she wanted.

"I'd forgotten how it felt, but Mrs. Yoshida became the mother I lost. It was like I was emotionally starved, and everyone was more than willing to support me." Hajime's arms tightened around her. He wasn't surprised that his mother stepped up and chose to mother Reina. Yuuka Yoshida was a special woman, someone who was always ready to love but could be firm enough to make sure of discipline. It made Hajime happy to discover Reina also benefited from Yuuka Yoshida's form of mothering.

"I'd often find myself sitting in front of my grandmother while she'd brush out my hair. My grandfather and uncle would let me help out at Amai Omoide in the kitchen, letting me watch them, and eventually… teaching me everything."

"Is that when you started your training in making wagashi in earnest?" Hajime asked in a whisper, looking down at her face. He saw Reina smile as she nodded.

"Your dad would always give me a pat on the head, helped me with some of my projects and patiently explained subjects I had a hard time understanding. I transferred to the school Tatsu attended, and things started to go back to normal. Tatsu asked me to be his language partner in both French and Japanese writing. Itsuki and Masashi helped me with math and science, also took the time to help me prepare for my university exams. Alongside my uncle and grandparents, your family supported me during school festivals or whenever I had volleyball games. Tatsu would be one of my loudest cheerleaders, and I made sure to always cheer for him during his football games."

Hajime was in awe as he listened to Reina recount all the things every single member of his family had done for her. He briefly wonderful what he would have done had he returned to Japan earlier, or if he had continued his higher education on Japanese soil.

The thought was fleeting as Hajime was aware there was no changing the past.

"I was really quiet at first. On one of my many check-ups, Uncle Ichigo and my grandparents broached the topic with my doctor. He recommended that I speak with a professional but made it clear that it is only if I was comfortable. No one forced me to go. I didn't want to go because I was scared. Then one day, I got tired of being afraid so I started opening up to my uncle. He didn't react outwardly to what I was saying. I could though tell he was affected when I told him the times Mr. Suzuki hit me or other things I experienced in Tokyo. He'd only patted me on head, like he always did when I was a child and told me, "you're home now." It took time to readjust…to process…that I was back home here in Kyoto and things were going to be okay. It also took time to heal physically and emotionally."

"I'm happy that you talked with your uncle about it," Hajime commented. He knew by experience how terrible it was if those kinds of negative experiences and emotions are left to fester inside. It would have caused more damage than the initial incident. He shuddered just thinking about how it would have destroyed Reina from the inside.

"Talking with Uncle Ichigo, we eventually talked about my mom. I told him about my anger and confusion…how she could change…everything. I wanted nothing to do with my mother. Uncle Ichigo patiently listened to me. But he asked me one simple question, "are your decisions fuelled by anger?" He told me it is quite understandable to feel what I was feeling, but he never affirmed or denied my feelings." Reina shifted her position and looked up at Hajime, who looked back at her. "When I confirmed that it was anger talking, Uncle Ichigo told me if I start letting anger control my life, I might be allowing myself to live a life full of bitterness and possible regrets."

"From the sounds of it your uncle encouraged you to forgive your mom."

"Not necessarily. He just wanted me to let go of the anger. For me, it was letting go of the hatred by learning how to forgive. I didn't do it for Mom or even Mr. Suzuki. I did it for me." Reina answered. She could remember how painstaking the process of letting go had been. She often reflected on it during the quietness of the night, when she would try finding sleep. She eventually came to the realisation that no matter what happened, Reika was still her mother. No matter what her actions had been, it didn't change the fact that she was her mom. As the child of Reika and Yuuki Maruyama, there would always be a part of her that loved her mom. It was then she remembered her promise to her father. She had doubts so she talked with her uncle once more.

"It took me time to forgive but I still hesitated. I didn't want to. I told my uncle my dad would understand if I didn't reach out to my mom after everything that happened. Uncle Ichigo agreed that my dad would have understood. That was the end of it. But after a while, I started asking myself if I still loved my mother...after everything she put me through...and the answer was a 'yes'."

"Did that sway you to finally send something to your mom?" Hajime couldn't help but ask.

Reina shook her head. "I debated within myself – trying to figure out what was the right thing to do. I wanted to honour my promise to my dad but at the same time, I told myself to never forget what I went through. In the end, I decided to reach out." Reina could remember reading something in a book. She had forgotten what book it was, or what they story was about but she could remember one small thing about it – a particular line that went, "*...you cannot give what you do not have.*" She wanted to get in touch – even just to let her mother know that Reina had forgiven her.

"I started to send messages to Mom...for Dad...for me...just like I promised him on his deathbed. I started greeting her during holidays, her birthday, at random to ask her how she was...to tell her that I was doing better in school...when I passed my university test…little things. The messages would always say *read*, but she would never answer. When I visited Tokyo recently, I told her about it, hoping she'd want to meet up with me. But…she never replied."

"That's highly commendable on your part, but can I say I don't like knowing you experience more and more disappointment every time you send something." Hajime commented. He reached over and tucked Reina's hair behind her ear.

"I'm actually very close to giving up," Reina admitted.

"No one will blame you if you stopped," Hajime reassured. "You are within your rights to do so. You can say that you've done what you could."

"Well, we will see how long my stubborn streak will hold out," Reina replied to break the melancholy around them. Hajime snorted, which led to the both of them laughing.

Reina took a breath before continuing, "Coming home to Kyoto also saved me, Hajime. I understand how healing it was to move back after something so…heartbreaking." She looked up at him then. "There are still dark days, but more than this place, the people here make it easier to bear. You've gone through something I know will never go away…you're learning to live with it. But if you do have your dark days, I'll be right here beside you. Thank you for sharing the truth with me. When the nightmare escapes that box where I'm sure you're keeping it inside your mind, you don't have to talk about it. But if you'd like to talk about it, I'll listen."

CHAPTER 13

A lot of things were revealed between the two of them. Even though they had talked about the dark experiences they've had, the silence that enveloped them was peaceful. Both Reina and Hajime felt that there was a shift in their relationship – closer...more intimate. Sitting beside each other on the couch with their hands locked together, neither of the two felt the need to break the silence.

The revelations they shared with one another brought with them complicated emotions that were difficult to process. They were things neither expected the other to have experienced.

Reina thought her experiences weren't as grave as with Hajime went through. She wondered if she could truly support Hajime. She was quick to dismiss that thought and reprimanded herself for being foolish. She loved Hajime and would do her best to love him and help him if he needed it. So lost in thought, she didn't realise that Hajime was studying the expressions playing out on her face.

"What are those expressions for?" Reina startled at Hajime's unexpected question. Her brows curled in a frown in confusion, as she tilted her head to the side. She wondered if she missed something he said.

Hajime laughed as he ran a finger between Reina's eyebrows, effectively stopping her frown. "You looked like you were contemplating something, which quickly morphed into concern and then, reprimand. Now, it's confusion," he said, sharing his observation. He watched as Reina's expression shifted again to soft smile.

"Nothing really," She replied. "If I can be perfectly honest, I'm relieved that you know the entire truth about the events that brought me back to Kyoto permanently."

Hajime nodded as he lifted the hand he was holding and laid a kiss on it. "I feel the same way about you knowing my story. We both found our way home, huh," he watched the smile on Reina's face bloom wider.

***

At the same moment in France...

Felipe opened the apartment door, his face white. His two roommates, Alexandre and Raphael, looked up from the dinner table. Judging by Felipe's expression, the brothers knew something was wrong.

Felipe pulled the empty chair and sat. He still hadn't said anything.

Raphael couldn't take it anymore. "What's wrong with you?"

"I met up with some friends who're still employed at the restaurant Hajime and I worked at," Felipe explained.

The brothers looked at each other again. A sense of foreboding came over them. As a lawyer, Alexandre took over the questioning. "From your expression, I take it it's something bad. What is happening this time?"

"After what they did to Hajime, the restaurant we worked at has been facing a lot of serious problems, to the point that it is barely surviving. I wasn't the only one who left. The two who did stay are about to submit their resignation letter because there hasn't been work. They are paid, yes, but it's minimum pay since the restaurant is closed. The only reason the restaurant still somewhat exists is Pierre. To be fair with him, he does have his own money – a significant amount from what everyone presumes. It pains me to see something

Emily and Arnaud spent their lives nurturing slowly die out. They were good people," Felipe answered.

"The silver lining I can see is that Emily and Arnaud at no longer with us to witness what is happening to their legacy," Raphael commented.

Felipe nodded. He wholeheartedly agreed. He had high respect for the couple. "Yeah. I would have been extra painful to see both heartbroken," he paused before continuing with the news he had heard, "I was told Juliette broke off her engagement with Pierre."

Raphael frowned. "They weren't engaged long," he turned to his brother and asked, "When was the last time you saw her?"

"The last meeting with the mediator for the settlement about a month and a half ago. I vaguely remember Juliette sitting beside Pierre." Alexandre answered.

Pierre nodded. "I think every single one of the people who knows the pair speculated that they're only together because of the child. But," he leaned forward to grab a piece of bread from the breadbasket in the middle of the table. "I think it was more about financial security. As Emily's sole heir, he inherited all her estate – including the restaurant. But due to Hajime being fired, Hajime's settlement, our mass resignation, the ongoing criminal investigation for alleged money laundering and fraud, all assets related to Emily's estate is frozen. That means, the restaurant hasn't opened in a while. We all know that's like a deathblow to any business. It has left Pierre in a not as financially secure as he was. With paying for lawyers and the new baby, Juliette needs money. Apparently, Juliette is making some noise that she's planning to rekindle things with Hajime."

"Why?" Alexandre immediately asked. "Even if we disregard her alleged involvement in the illegal activity at the restaurant, she has slighted Hajime enough. Why would anyone want to get back with a former paramour knowing said former paramour cheated on you before?"

Felipe took a gulp of water. "Well said, my friend," he lifted his glass of water to toast Alexandre, "It's very difficult to truly understand how Juliette's mind works."

"Hajime has moved on with his life. I don't think the idea of getting back with her will be appealing to Hajime." Raphael never liked her. He tolerated her because he wanted to support his friend. But there was something about her that made him suspicious from the beginning.

"I'm agreeing with Felipe – she wants financial security. Pierre is out. I'm guessing she's banking on Hajime's character. She knows that if she can somehow persuade Hajime to take her back, there would be no question as to him supporting her and the child. I know that she had helped Hajime make some good investments here in France through the bank. I doubt she's above using her own baby to soften Hajime's heart – make him out as a bleeding heart," Alexandre said.

"Right you are," Felipe answered, pointing a finger in Alexandre's direction. "I think we can all agree that not one of us trusts Juliette. She's not above manipulating anyone or anything to get what she wants. She's not one to care who gets hurts as long as she gets what she wants."

"I'll add a warning when I call him next to update him on the settlement money and the criminal case. Immediate steps can stop this nonsense." Alexandre said.

***

1863, Third year of Bunkyuu, Edo Period

Riku and Shiori started to fully appreciate the protection offered by the Satsuma when political tension arose in Kyoto a few months after that fateful night. As commoners, they weren't privy to the affairs of the imperial court and the shogunate. But it didn't take much effort to realise there was something different. Something was going on.

The various samurai factions were increasingly agitated and more vigilant. Riku and Shiori had learned to pay attention to warriors' non-verbal cues back in their home village. It was a skill that served them well.

The samurai that visited their shop to buy some sweets were cordial and polite. As of late, the newly minted Shinsengumi were seen around their area. Some of their members came into the shop to buy sweets. The Shinsengumi – a small and elite group of swordsmen - didn't have a good reputation around Kyoto. The group had been commissioned initially by the military government for protection. Given the political climate of Kyoto, the group sent a letter to the Aizu clan, a powerful clan who supported the Tokugawa regime, for permission to police the streets of Kyoto. Upon the granting of the request, the group was given the name of Shinsengumi by the lord of the Aizu clan.

The Shinsengumi members were looked down upon due to their common or low-ranking samurai background. Their association with the Aizu clan didn't help their reputation as the Aizu was an opposing force against the Choshu and Satsuma clans.

Riku and Shiori treated any Shinsengumi member who ventured into the store just like any customer. They decided to be respectful and kind.

But naturally the atmosphere turned cold when Satsuma members and Shinsengumi ventured into the shop at the same time. When the Shinsengumi realised that Amai Omoide was under Satsuma protection, their visits dwindled and eventually stopped. Riku and Shiori would still see them walking around, and when one of them was outside sweeping, the Shinsengumi were cordial enough but mostly left them alone.

They started having trouble with some Choshu samurai and ronin employed by Choshu supporters. The couple eventually learned through the grapevine that the Choshu clan was driven out from the imperial court by the Tokugawa, Aizu, and Satsuma clans in late September 1863. While they didn't really understand the reason why Choshu was forced out, Riku and Shiori knew it was serious enough that a new kind of tension was settling in Kyoto.

Winter was about to start again. The leaves had already changed colour and the last of them had started falling. They'd had a few incidents with the Choshu, and they were just getting over them. They only involved some rude language and eventual dismissal by the Choshu, but Riku and Shiori didn't want trouble, so they chose not to escalate and didn't notify the Satsuma when it first happened. But word slowly reached the Satsuma anyway.

Knowing the Choshu would likely retaliate and scheme against them, the Satsuma clan took every rumour seriously. They sent people to investigate around Amai Omoide but decided not to make a move until it was necessary.

On one particular day, Kouki was playing outside while his mother had Akito strapped to her back. She had been sweeping fallen leaves into piles, and her husband was inside the shop preparing more confections for the afternoon.

Shiori was humming a soft song to lull her youngest son to sleep. It was a peaceful day, and they had just finished lunch. Both parents wanted Kouki to use up a little bit more energy before his afternoon nap.

The peace suddenly ended with their eldest son's cry. Shiori quickly looked over at her son and froze when she saw him on the ground cowering before a huge man. Samurai. Based on the crest on his clothing and those with him, they were from the Choshu clan.

Shiori immediately ran and knelt in front of her son and begged the man, "I apologise for my son. He's just a young boy. Please forgive him."

The man sneered and drew his sword. Shiori paled but shielded her sons.

"That brat was in the way and hit me. It seems that as his mother, you need to be taught to stay out of your betters' way so that your children too may learn. Or perhaps do away with the brat all together." He raised his sword.

Shiori closed her eyes and extended both arms in a feeble attempt to protect her sons. She wouldn't turn her body knowing full well that Akito would be struck. She could only wait for her demise and silently prayed that the men would spare her children.

The blow never came. When Shiori peaked, she was stunned to see one of the men she'd patched up had deflected the katana meant for her and her children. She was shaken out of her thoughts when another pair of hands grasped her upper arms and hauled her up. Her scream got stuck on her throat when she saw it was the other samurai she had helped.

"Take your sons inside and don't come out," he instructed as he motioned her towards the entrance of Amai Omoide.

He immediately drew his sword and faced the Choshu men. As Shiori took Kouki's hand and all but dragged him into the shop, she looked back and noticed for the first time that the two Satsuma samurai weren't alone. More of them had arrived as they clashed with the Choshu.

Without another thought, Shiori barred herself and her children inside the shop.

***

After finishing their last exam, Reina, Aika, and Aika's boyfriend, Ryo, walked from campus together, excited about the start of their winter vacation. As they neared the university gates, Aika nudged Reina with her elbow and looked towards the gates.

Reina followed her best friend's gaze. When she realised who was there waiting for her, a beautiful smile spread on her face. She turned quickly to Aika to excuse herself, but her best friend was way ahead of her.

"Go on. I'll catch you later," said Aika.

Reina nodded and wished both of them a good afternoon. Then, she made her way towards Hajime.

When Hajime noticed Reina, he stood straight and waited patiently for her. As Reina walked towards him, he offered a bow towards Aika and the man whom he presumed to be her boyfriend, and they reciprocated the gesture. He smiled as Reina stopped in front of him.

Without preamble, Hajime reached out and took Reina's school bag from her, carrying it as they both started walking towards the station.

Aika observed her best friend and her boyfriend. There was a time where she thought Reina and Tatsunori would end up together, but when she really scrutinized their interactions, there was never more than a sibling relationship with those them. Aika hadn't had the chance to interact with Hajime much as with Tatsunori, but she could see the mutual respect and deep friendship he and Reina had. In her opinion, that was a solid foundation to build on. Aika felt jubilant seeing Reina happy.

CHAPTER 14

1864, First year of Genji, Edo Period

When Riku and Shiori moved to Kyoto, they'd both wanted a fresh start. They didn't have much choice, but they'd hoped it would be more peaceful than where they'd come from. They forgot to take into account Kyoto was the centre of politics, which meant there was always something going on.

It had been a blessing that they were taken under Satsuma protection. It seemed that in order to survive and live in relative peace in the capital, you should be careful who you associate with.

The Choshu left them alone for the most part after the last violent encounter in front of Amai Omoide. The unit of the Satsuma samurai the Maruyama couple had helped had made a strong statement that day: Amai Omoide was under Satsuma protection.

While their affiliation with Satsuma gave them more security, it also affected their circle of friends. Some shop owners and families stopped interacting with them or treated them with hostility. Riku and Shiori weren't sure if the cause was fear, jealousy, or mere misunderstanding that drove their neighbours' behaviour.

In the end, Riku and Shiori learned to take it with a grain of salt. If that was what it meant to live in the capital, they would adapt.

But things didn't settle down after the Choshu clash the year before. About a month ago, in early July, word spread widely across Kyoto that the Shinsengumi had arrested a lot of shishi in what was now being called the Ikedaya incident.

From the grapevine, Riku and Shiori found out that the shishi was a group of political activists. They comprised of mostly masterless samurai who were formerly associated with different domains like Choshu, Tosa, and Higo. They were said to an anti-Tokugawa group.

Based on the stories, it was a violent clash. Rumours claimed that the Choshu had planned to burn Kyoto, and the Shinsengumi were able to stop them. Others were saying that it was only Nakagawa-no-miya, Prince Nakagawa, that was being targeted to be burned. Yet others claimed that the meeting at Ikedaya was simply where Choshu members were to talk about how to rescue a shishi member who had strong ties with the Choshu.

Regardless of the true intent of the shishi Ikedaya meeting, the incident elevated the popularity of the Shinsengumi and attracted new recruits. However, it didn't dispel the tension in the capital.

What started out as a normal day quickly turned into chaos. Riku and Shiori were serving customers when suddenly, screaming and ruckus were heard from outside. People froze, then started panicking when the distinct smell of smoke reached them.

Customers fled the store, running in every direction. Riku instructed Shiori to get the two boys from the back, and his wife immediately obeyed. These were almost exact same circumstances that drove them to the capital.

The Maruyama couple ran out of the shop with their two children. Akito was clinging to his mother while Kouki held his father's hand. They halted they moment they got outside. Kyoto was burning.

Riku tried to see where it was safe to run. Fire was spreading around them quickly. Even through his panic, Riku noticed that the small path that led to a larger street behind their home. There were a lot of people on the larger street running away from the flames. The small alleyway wouldn't remain safe to cross for long. He turned to his wife. "Run! Take the children through this path! It should lead out of town."

"But—" Shiori tried to reason with her husband, fear consuming her.

"There is no time! This place is about to burn! All our stores and homes are made of wood. Anything made of wood is getting caught up in the fire! There are a lot of old people who won't be able to run like us. I need to help control the fire."

"The fire is spreading too quickly!"

"I know, Shiori," Riku answered calmly as he passed Kouki's hand to his wife. "It might be impossible, but we need to do something to help. We ran once and watched our village burn. I won't do that again. But I need you and the children to be safe. Soaking the unburned houses will slow down the spread if not prevent more burning. But hurry, Shiori! Go!" With that, Riku started running towards the end of the block to gather as many men as he could.

Shiori could feel tears form in her eyes, wiping them away before her children saw. She needed to be strong, especially for her children. Strengthening her resolve, she turned around and started running with her children in her arms.

***

Reina and Hajime had gone out for dinner, enjoying some of the winter light displays during their walk after their meal. They were engaged in a debate regarding Christmas lights, discussing the pros and cons of vibrant multi-coloured lights or simple white lights.

Hajime's phone started ringing. He intended to let the call go to voicemail, but when the first call ended and another immediately started, Reina smiled and told him to answer.

When Hajime realised that the call was from France, a part of him was apprehensive. His friends would usually send him a message first to make sure that he was free.

"Good afternoon, Alexandre. How are you?" Hajime greeted his friend.

"Good evening, my friend. How are you? Aside from Felipe being annoying at times, we are still the same."

Hajime laughed as he made eye contact with Reina. She smiled back and walked a few steps away to give him privacy. But before she could step away, Hajime grabbed her hand. Reina tilted her head to the side and raised an eyebrow.

Hajime smiled and pulled her over. "Alexandre, let's switch to a video call. I'd like to introduce you to a special someone." Reina blushed, having understood what Hajime was telling his friend. Hajime turned his video on and positioned his phone so that both he and Reina were in frame. "Alexandre, I'd like you to meet Reina, my girlfriend. Rei, this is Alexandre, one of my closest friends in France."

Reina smiled and waved. "It's nice to meet you, Alexandre. Hajime has told me about you and your other roommates."

"It's wonderful to meet you, mademoiselle. A beauty like you… what are you doing with Hajime?"

Reina laughed as she looked up at Hajime, who raised an eyebrow. "He's not perfect, true, but I'm not either. Besides, he's a wonderful partner who makes me feel like I can get through the worst of things." Hajime's eyes softened as he gave her a gentle smile.

"Ah, young love," Alexandre commented.

"You and Raphael are only a few months older than me," Hajime remarked. "Anyway, you usually send me a message or email before calling. Is something the matter?"

Alexandre paused. It was a delicate issue that he was sure was going to hurt not just his friend but also his new girlfriend. Knowing that Reina could understand French, he decided to exercise caution. "Um, it's a sensitive issue. No offence, Reina, but Hajime, are you sure you'd like to have her hear it?"

"There are no secrets between us," Hajime replied. There was no hesitance. Alexandre could tell that his friend was comfortable with his answer. There was no tightening of his jaw or change in body language.

"Even if it might hurt her?"

"Is it about Hajime's previous job or his ex-girlfriend?" Rayna asked. She liked Hajime's friend and appreciated that he seemed to be looking out not only for Hajime but for her too. "If it's related to either of those, I'm fine, Alexandre. I promised Hajime that I'll weather any storm with him, no matter how uncomfortable or hurtful. We promised to face the truth together." She looked up at Hajime and gave him a smile.

Both looked to the camera and Hajime confirmed, "It is all right, Alexandre. Thank you for your concern, especially your regard towards Reina."

Alexandre liked Hajime's new girlfriend more and more. The camera did nothing to hide the love that reflected in each of their eyes. As an attorney, he could say that he had met his fair share of people. He could pick up a lot of things just by watching their non-verbal cues. There was nothing but love, respect, and openness coming from the couple he was talking with.

Taking a deep breath, Alexandre started updating Hajime about his pending case against his former employer. Alexandre had sued the company on Hajime's behalf – which had already been settled- and, was handling the embezzlement case against the same company, with Hajime and the former employees as his witnesses. He then went on to warn Hajime of what Felipe had told him about Juliette.

Hajime and Reina looked at each other. Reina gave him an encouraging nod. Hajime looked back to his friend and said, "What do you need me to do, Alexandre?"

***

After hanging up with Alexandre, Hajime took hold of Reina's hand and led her to the nearest bench.

"Talk to me, Rei. How do you really feel?"

Reina sighed and closed her eyes. She squeezed Hajime's hand. "I appreciated Alexandre's concern. It's frustrating. I don't understand why she would like to drag you into her mess. Is she aware you are in Japan now? Does she even know your Japanese address?" Hajime ran his thumb over her fingers as she spoke.

He let out a sigh. "I did mention once that I am from Kyoto. I never told her my parents' address and I could care less what she knows or doesn't know. If she knows I am in Japan, she didn't hear it from me or any of my friends. I don't maintain any social media accounts aside from the Japanese app my brothers made me download even while I was in France." Reina leaned her head against Hajime's left shoulder. "I've known Juliette for years but only had a short three-month romantic relationship with her. Things started to get sour on our second month. I started having suspicions about her. I finally had enough of her behaviour last New Year. It might sound cold, but I broke it off on New Year's Day."

Reina leaned back and smiled. "I don't think anyone should judge you when you ended the relationship. I'm just happy you got out of a toxic relationship."

Hajime chuckled. "Perhaps. I'm glad I never introduced her to my family."

"Hmm. Mrs. Yoshida would have been vocal about her opinion about Juliette had you introduced her."

A moment of silence passed between the two of them before Hajime looked to Reina. "I'm sorry if my past—"

"Pardon me for cutting you off, Hajime, but please don't apologise. It's true that you were in a relationship with Juliette before. I won't compete with that past. It's pointless. Whatever things you talked about or did together, ultimately, they still brought you home to me. Her actions now are her own. The legal cases you are involved in aren't because you are at fault. Someone else unfairly decided to involve you. I'm glad you have Alexandre representing you. Now, I am choosing to stand beside you, Hajime."

Words could be very powerful indeed. Hajime tucked a stray hair behind Reina's ear. "I have fallen in love with someone so strong.

As much as I wish this didn't affect you, I understand it cannot be helped. Thank you for choosing to be with me. I promise you I'll work hard to be worthy enough to stand beside you."

Reina smiled and gave a nod of acknowledgement. "I'm happy you have friends, aside from Alexandre, in France who continue to look out for you."

Hajime couldn't help but laugh. He too was grateful. "They are interesting characters, but I wouldn't trade them for the world."

"Why don't we send them our Christmas greetings then? Like a picture of us, and we could edit it and add a short message," Reina suggested.

"Why not? The background here looks nice for a Christmas-themed greeting," Hajime answered as he took his phone out again, and they smiled for the camera.

***

Alexandre arrived home to see his brother getting ready to leave for his shift while Felipe cooked in the kitchen.

"I talked with Hajime," Alexandre said as he placed his briefcase down and removed his coat and suit jacket.

"How'd it go?" Felipe asked, not turning around from his cooking.

Alexandre got a wine glass and poured himself some wine. "He took it better than expected actually." He took a sip before adding, "His girlfriend was a huge support."

His brother and Felipe stopped what they were doing and looked towards Alexandre.

"You met his girlfriend?" Raphael asked.

Alexandre nodded. "She's the polar opposite of Juliette. She stood by Hajime when I updated him."

"Wow," Raphael commented just as Felipe asked, "You don't happen to have a picture of her, do you?"

"They took a photo together and send it along with some Christmas greetings." Alexandre took his phone out and brought up the picture Hajime sent.

Felipe and Raphael both walked behind Alexandre to peer at a picture of Hajime and Reina smiling at the camera with the beautiful lights as their backdrop. Accompanying it was a simply message:

Merry Christmas! Wishing you a wonderful holiday from Japan.

Felipe leaned closer to study the picture. When he straightened, he commented, "Hajime has changed. I'm glad."

Alexandre nodded. "There's a lot of love and respect between them. I'm glad he has someone who isn't afraid to fight for him when things get tough."

"Hajime's going to need someone like her to overcome the challenges of life," Raphael commented as he went to grab his stuff to head out for work. Then, he said to Alexandre, "I hope you do something about that."

"Oh, don't worry. I already have a plan," Alexandre answered his brother.

CHAPTER 15

1866, Second year of Keio, Edo Period

It took a long time to rebuild after the Kinmon incident. Much of Kyoto burned, but due to valiant efforts by a few like Riku, they were able to save some neighbourhoods. They worked tirelessly to douse as much of the fire as they could while also making sure it didn't spread.

While much of the bloody encounters happened near the imperial palace at the Hamaguri—the Forbidden Gate—there were also a lot of civilian casualties, especially those who weren't able to escape the fire.

Not even a day later, word spread that the Choshu were responsible for the rebellion. A few months after that, the shogunate ordered a retaliation against the Choshu. The Satsuma, led by Takamori Saigo, headed the Choshu expedition. Further bloodshed was avoided when Takamori Saigo negotiated to avoid fighting and for the Choshu to surrender the three people behind the attack against the imperial palace. The issue was resolved when the three committed seppuku.

Riku had been injured during the Kinmon incident. There were burn marks on his hands from when he'd grabbed a piece of burning wood to try to save someone. While he had been successful, the burns were bad.

When he reunited with Shiori and the children, Shiori burst into tears. It had been a mixture of relief and fear. She didn't remember much of what happened during the next few days as she nursed her husband while also keeping the store going. Whenever she could, she would help out their neighbours, giving food or offering to do their groceries.

Kouki, seeing his mother's determination and having heard about his father's efforts, tagged along with his mother at the tender age of four to see if there was anything he could do,

When his father started getting back on his feet, he decided to help him around the kitchen, fetching materials or ingredients while his father tried to work with his hands.

There was a sense of community in their part of Kyoto. The families that Riku had saved extended a helping hand to him and his family whenever they could.

Touma Yamashita and Takashi Higashi, the two Satsuma samurai the Maruyama family share mutual respect with, had also been constant sources of support.

Touma Yamashita had offered some Western medicine to help with Riku's recovery. Both Riku and Shiori knew that it must have cost a lot. They told him it was unnecessary, but Touma insisted that it was nothing. They had saved his life before, bringing him back from the brink of death. The ointment was only a fraction of what the couple deserved.

His younger brother, Keisuke, had exhibited incredible intelligence and was sent by the Satsuma to Europe to be educated. He gravitated towards medicine. Since coming back to Kagoshima, Keisuke had been instrumental in improving the medical system in their domain. When he had learned that Touma had been saved by the daughter of a village doctor, he waited for the perfect opportunity to repay her and her husband for saving his brother.

That moment came when he received word from Touma about Riku's burns immediately after the Choshu expedition. He was tied up with obligations within the Satsuma domain, so he couldn't go check on Riku himself. However, knowing Riku's wife had some medical background, he sent the burn ointment he'd prepared.

When things at the capital settled a little after the Choshu expedition, Touma was able to travel back to Kagoshima for a visit and take a short break from duty. It was then that Touma fully explained how Riku came about his injuries. Keisuke admired the humble man and the resilience of his wife.

Keisuke had wanted to meet the couple, so he made sure that he can take the time away from his responsibilities without problems and accompanied Touma back to the capital. He wasn't disappointed when he met them. When Riku and Shiori found out that he was the one who had created the salve, they thanked him profusely, but Keisuke immediately offered to give Riku a check-up in response. The couple had wanted to pay him, but he adamantly refused. It was then that Riku crafted a special assortment of sweets, and Shiori packed it in a lacquer box—red on the inside, black on the outside with gold embellishments.

The lacquer itself was quite expensive, and the confections were exquisite. Keisuke accepted the offering.

Over the years, he too became more acquainted with the Maruyama family. During the last days of April 1866, Keisuke heard some rumours that the Satsuma were now working with Choshu. It was said that it was only a matter of time before they overthrew the Tokugawa shogunate.

Touma had been busy, so Keisuke didn't bother to ask for details. Instead, he sent a letter to Touma to inform him that he'd be heading to Kyoto to invite the Maruyama couple to stay at Satsuma for a while.

It was early May when Keisuke arrived in front of Amai Omoide. The children, Kouki and Akito, were the first to spot him.

"Good morning, Dr. Yamashita." *Kouki bowed as he greeted the doctor. His younger brother followed his example.*

"Good morning, Kouki, Akito. Are your parents inside?"

"Yes, Dr. Yamashita. They are finishing the first batches of sweets for the day. Akito and I will be helping as soon as we finish sweeping the front," *Kouki explained.*

The man smiled and gave a nod. "Do you mind if I go visit with them?"

"Akito, tell Father and Mother that Dr. Yamashita is here," *Kouki ordered his younger brother, who was more than happy to comply.*

Keisuke smiled. The two youngsters were growing fast. He knew they'd already experienced a lot, which pushed them to mature quicker.

It wasn't long before Riku and Shiori came to greet him. Both bowed and welcomed him inside.

"Pardon my intrusion this morning, Riku. I should have sent word at least," Keisuke said as he sat at the table Riku had led him to. "Also, congratulations. It seems like you two are expecting more blessings." He gestured towards Shiori's swollen belly as she was making tea.

Riku smiled towards his wife. "It was a surprise but a blessing, nonetheless. My wife is hoping that we get a girl this time."

"Either a son or a daughter, I will love this new little one the same," Shiori commented as she offered a cup of tea to Keisuke. She then laid a loving hand on her stomach.

Keisuke took a sip of the tea and gestured that the two sit with him. "Have you two heard of satsumaimo?"

Riku and Shiori looked at each other before Riku answered, "Yes but neither of us have tried it yet."

Keisuke smiled and said, "In Satsuma, when we say satsumaimo, we mean the sweet potato with reddish skin and white centres. I have a patient who produces different kinds of sweet potatoes — from the traditional satsumaimo; murasaki sweet potatoes that have a purple skin and white centres that turn golden when cooked; and, the white skinned and purple centred ones. I'd be more than happy to introduce you if you are interested in adding a sweet potato-based item on your menu — perhaps just as roasted sweet potato or as an ingredient of kuri kinton for the traditional New Year's Day food."

"We are grateful, Dr. Yamashita, but you don't have to go out of your way," Shiori replied.

A certain look came over Keisuke's face as he looked down at his cup of tea. "I chose to become a doctor because unlike my brothers, I have a different skill set. What you both did for Touma is something my family and I will forever be grateful for." He then looked up towards the couple. There was a severity in his gaze that got Riku and Shiori sitting straight.

"Something will happen in Kyoto in the near future—in a few weeks, or perhaps a few months. You and your family have already gone through a lot. Please let me extend this invitation to my home in Kagoshima where you can stay while we all weather through the upcoming storm.

"While there, you can learn more about our regional speciality, the sweet potato, establish contacts, suppliers, everything you need to add it to your menu if or when you decide to return to Kyoto. You have two young children and another on the way. Please let me and my family offer you safety."

***

Reina finished preparing the kuri kinton as part of their New Year's meal. Her grandmother and Hajime's mother had helped with the rest of the dishes for their osechi that year. Not a lot of people prepared osechi at home anymore and would rather order from a restaurant or buy it at the supermarket. Reina understood her family's preference for preparing theirs. It would have been convenient to buy it, but Reina enjoyed the preparation process. It was always filled with stories and laughter.

It was a joy to make something special for the family. With that said, she didn't begrudge others for their choices. She had to admit that preparing osechi was a lot of work. For her, though, it was more than food. It was the nostalgia and the warmth the process brought. It was one of the things her grandmother had taught her when she returned to Kyoto. Spending time in the kitchen while Yuzuki shared stories from when her father and uncle were kids were some of her favourite memories.

Reina turned to help Hajime and Tatsunori with the rest of their New Year's meal. Tatsunori was preparing toshikoshi soba while Hajime was busy preparing chocolate decorations to go with the desserts Reina was making.

Hajime and Reina had agreed that they'd serve a special daifuku for the family. Tossing some ideas between them, they eventually decided to make it look like a kagami mochi. They wanted to try a combination of fruits like nashi pear, grapes, and persimmon but agreed that it sounded too sweet, so they used dark chocolate for the filling. For the topmost layer, they decided to mix yuzu and mandarin pulp into the rice flour, and then shape the ball into a mandarin. Reina modelled the inside to also look like an orange, and Hajime coated the outside with orange coloured chocolate.

They experimented on ratios before the New Year until they were satisfied with the taste. Reina also experimented with the tea. Since it was a non-traditional daifuku, she knew that simple green tea would not fully fit the taste profile they were aiming for. She had prepared the tea leaves and the filling beforehand, and Hajime had finished the mandarins earlier. All that was left was to prepare the mochi.

"Need any help in here?" Masashi asked as he headed to the sink to wash his hands.

"Finished with the preparations for hatsumode, Masashi?" Tatsunori asked about their first shrine visit of the year.

"Yes. Itsuki and Dad are just doing the final checks but all in all, our shrine is ready for hatsumode." Masashi walked over to Tatsunori. "Need help?"

"Yeah, sure. The assembly is the only thing left. I'm just about done with the noodles," Tatsunori said.

Masashi nodded as he took out the bowls they'd use.

"Masashi, if it isn't too much trouble, could you also please bring out the cups for tea?"

"No problem. Do you need me to turn on the kettle?" Masashi could see that Reina still had her hands full of mochi. Although it looked like she was almost done, he didn't mind helping her out too.

"Yes, please! Thanks, Masashi." Reina smiled.

***

Ichigo was sitting with his parents and Yuuka at the table. The osechi boxes were ready for New Year's Day. He couldn't help but glance at his niece with the three Yoshida boys.

"How's the rehab going, Ichigo?" Yuuka asked, bringing him back to the present.

He turned and smiled. "It's going really well. After the New Year, I'll be visiting my primary doctor again for a check-up, but according to my physical therapist, my muscles are regaining their strength well. I might be cleared to graduate from my wheelchair soon."

The Yoshida matriarch couldn't help but exclaim, "That's great news!"

"Yes, we are relieved that he's progressing really well," Kouji, Ichigo's father, commented.

His wife, Yuzuki, couldn't help but smile. As a mother, there weren't enough words that could express her relief. She had already buried one son. She didn't want to lose another. "Before long, you'll be with us in the kitchen again." She patted her son's hand on the table.

"That would be nice, Mom. I do miss being able to work," Ichigo admitted. "But it's also nice to take a step back and watch what the next generation is doing."

All looked towards the kitchen. They watched as Reina, Hajime, and Masashi stilled and turned towards Tatsunori. As if realising what he'd said, Tatsunori blushed and gestured wildly with his hands. Reina, Hajime, and Masashi burst out laughing.

"Ah! Well, isn't that a wonderful sight to see and hear," Issei commented as he, his eldest son and his wife - Itsuki and Haruka - walked up to the table. Issei laid a hand on his wife, Yuuka's shoulder. "What a good way to welcome the New Year."

"Yes, it is." Ichigo agreed.

Tatsunori and Masashi started bringing out the bowls, closely followed by Reina and Hajime. The table might've been cramped, and some of them had to eat on the kitchen counter, but it was a dinner with a lot of teasing, laughter, and stories.

While Issei, Yuuka, Itsuki, and Haruka changed in preparation for hatsumode, Tatsunori offered to wash the dishes. Without a word, Reina and Hajime followed to help him while Masashi stayed with Reina's grandparents and uncle.

CHAPTER 16

Reina's phone started ringing. She took her phone out of her pocket, wondering who was calling. It was too early for a New Year's greeting. Reina's heart leapt to her throat. The number that was flashing on her screen was from the police station.

"I'll be in your childhood bedroom, Hajime. I need to answer this call," she said as a quick explanation, heading towards his room without waiting for a reply. Hajime and Tatsunori shared a look, both were curious about Reina's hasty actions.

"Good evening," Reina answered as soon as she breached her boyfriend's room. She quietly closed the door behind her but didn't walk further into the room.

"Good evening. Is this Reina Maruyama?"

"Yes, sir."

There was a pause. The man on the other end grew solemn. "Ms. Maruyama, this is Officer Sato. I suggest that you take a seat. I unfortunately have some grave news."

Reina stayed silent. She was frozen, mind reeling.

"Earlier tonight, Yuito Suzuki and Reika Suzuki were involved in an accident. Ms. Maruyama, I believe that Reika Suzuki is your mother, am I correct?"

"Y-yes, sir,"

"I am truly sorry to give you this news, Ms. Maruyama, especially since it's the New Year, but Yuito Suzuki passed away during the accident, and your mother, Reika Suzuki, passed away not long after arriving at the hospital."

Reina's knees buckled from under her. She slid to the floor and continued to listen with now cold fingers to the police officer on the other end of the line. Shock coursed through her veins. Her limbs were like jelly. It was impossible. Her mother couldn't have died mere hours ago.

***

Hajime was wiping his hands on a small towel as he and Tatsunori finished with the dishes. He looked to the direction of the hallway that led to the bedrooms. There was still no sign of Reina.

"Rei still hasn't come back," Tatsunori remarked.

Hajime nodded before handing the towel to his brother and said, "I'll go and check on her."

As he walked towards his childhood bedroom, he thought about Reina's reaction when she saw who was calling her. The surprise on her face was obvious. He also saw a flicker of fear on her eyes. The phone call worried Hajime. He couldn't help but wonder who called her. Standing outside his room's door, Hajime knocked before opening it, "Rei?"

Reina was on the floor, arms around her legs and face against her knees. Hajime was immediately at her side, kneeling. He placed a hand on her back, "Rei, what's wrong?"

"She's gone," her soft voice drifted to his ears.

Confusion entered Hajime's eyes. He could feel her back go up and down with her jagged breaths. "Who?" his voice was filled with his concern. His breath caught in his throat when he saw the devastation in her eyes as she lifted her head to make eye contact with him. Immense dread started filling his veins.

Reina's voice caught as she forced one word out, "Mom."

Hajime's body froze. His jaw dropped as his eyes grew wide. "Your mother?" he asked. His voice cracked.

"She's…dead…" Reina told him. Tears started falling uncontrollably. Heart wrenching sobs started to grip her entire body.

Hajime immediately pulled her to his chest and wrapped his arms around her. What could he say? What could any of them say? While Reina didn't share the same relationship he and his brothers did with their mother, Hajime knew she still loved her mother and tried her best to reach out. There weren't any words that could possibly make the situation better.

They sat on the floor, holding each other. Hajime wasn't sure how much time had passed before he decided to lift Reina and carry her over to the bed. He laid her down gently before laying down beside her and holding her close to his body. He started running his hand up and down her back to try and comfort her. He could feel the front of his shirt grow damper.

When Reina felt more in control of her grief, she started to share with him more about the phone call. "I was contacted by the police. He introduced himself as Officer Sato," she took a deep breath to help calm herself more, "There was a car accident earlier, which killed Mr. Suzuki immediately. Mom survived long enough to arrive at the hospital, but her injuries were grave. She didn't make it. Office Sato said that upon checking the records, my mother had filed a will in case of accidents. That's how he found my number. I was made my mother's emergency contact. He said that I do not need to worry about arrangements. Their bodies are being transported back to Tokyo as we speak. Officer Sato sent the address of the funeral home where they will be prepared for cremation."

Hajime tightened his embrace. "What do you want to do now? I'm sure you want to go to Tokyo." he whispered.

Reina leaned back, enough so she could look up at him. She used the sleeve of her sweater to wipe her eyes. With a nod, she then answered, "I need to tell my family. Everyone. But…" her voice trailed off as emotions threatened to overwhelm her again. "I don't think I can do it, Hajime."

"I can do it for you. Sounds good?" Hajime offered. With her nod, he added, "Why don't you stay here for a moment and rest while I go out there and tell them the news. Then, I'll come and get you so we can start heading to Tokyo."

"Thank you, Hajime."

"You are very welcome, love."

The kitchen was a mixture of activity and sound when Hajime re-entered. He could see his brothers, Masashi and Tatsunori, with Reina's relatives sharing a pot of tea. The other members of his family, Hajime assumed, were either still changing or outside.

Hajime walked up to the dining table and cleared his throat to catch everyone's attention. There wasn't an easy way to say what he needed. He took a steadying breath before starting, "Reina received a phone call earlier. It was from the police." The short statement was enough to cause an assortment of gasps, questions, and concerned looks directed at him. Hajime lifted a hand in a bid for silence before continuing, "Her mother and her husband met an accident earlier. They have both passed away." More gasps resounded but Hajime asked for more patience and silence, "Their bodies are on their way to Tokyo so Reina and I will be going."

Ichigo was heartbroken for his niece. He wheeled his wheelchair closer to Hajime and asked, "Where's Rei? How is she?"

Hajime gave a pained sigh. "She's in my room. I left her on the bed to rest. It's a huge shock and she's devastated as expected." Reina's expression and pained sobs were fresh in Hajime's mind. "At this point, I'm not sure if her mom's decision to make Reina her emergency contact is a blessing or a punishment."

Yuzuki wanted to be by her granddaughter's side and offer what comfort she could. Grief was something she wished her granddaughter didn't experience again in her young life. She had already lost a father. That night, she had lost her mother. There wasn't any possibility of reconciliation anymore. Death erased all that. Yuzuki stood and said, "I'll go and be with Reina." Hajime nodded and escorted her to his bedroom.

Inside Hajime's room, Reina turned and looked out the window. The sky was clear that night. The moon was full, with a spate of stars scatted throughout the black canvas of the night. Normally, Reina would have found peace looking at that scene. It was very difficult to find any trace of tranquillity as she was processing the information she was given. The silence of the room felt oppressive and claustrophobic. Reina squeezed her eyes shut, hoping for the foolish dream that it wasn't true her mother has passed that same evening. She furiously wiped away the few tears that escaped her eyes. It was so unfair! She had wanted so much to see and speak with her mother again, even just one time. It was never going to happen.

Reina didn't notice the door opening but felt the mattress dip behind her. A gentle hand landed on her shoulder before she heard the soft voice of her grandmother, calling her name "Rei." It broke another tenuous chain Reina had, a chain she was trying to use to contain the intense emotions she had in her heart. Reina shot up and wrapped her arms around her grandmother. She buried her face on her grandmother's shoulder, letting the older woman's familiar scent of sweets and roses envelope her battered heart with comfort and love. More sobs escaped Reina's lips as Yuzuki patted her granddaughter's head gently.

"I'm so sorry for the loss of your mother, sweetheart. Reika might have been out of your life for years, but it still doesn't lessen the pain of her death," Yuzuki softly spoken condolences served as a balm to Reina's aching heart. Her grandmother always had the right words that helped her cope.

"Hajime told us that your mom and Mr. Suzuki's bodies are being transported to Tokyo. I know it is painful, but I hope you get the chance to say goodbye properly to your mother and find peace with her death when you go," Yuzuki felt and saw Reina pulling away from her as she spoke. Gentle fingers that helped raise Reina slowly wiped tears from her granddaughter's face. "Do not worry about things here. Your family, with the help of Sayaka and Mio, is more than capable to taking over yours and Hajime's responsibilities towards Amai Omoide for hatsumode and the next couple of days. Simply take the time to grieve and say goodbye properly."

Hajime had watched the interaction in silence. He started to think about the things he needed to prepare before he and Reina headed to Tokyo. But before he could go into more planning about accommodations and such, Yuzuki stood from the bed, followed by Reina. Without any exchange of words, Hajime opened his arms as Reina walked towards him. After a quick embrace, all three left the room to find the others.

When the three re-entered the kitchen, Hajime's parents, his brothers, his sister-in-law, Reina's uncle and grandfather were convened. Everyone aside from Tatsunori were there. From everyone's shared expression of grief, Hajime knew someone had informed his parents, eldest brother and his wife about Reina's news. While the others approached Reina to offer an embrace and their condolences, Masashi had walked towards Hajime instead.

Hajime's second older brother said, "It's the New Year. It's impossible to book a train, plane, or bus tickets, let alone get a last-minute hotel reservation. Do not worry though. I've handled everything. I'll send all the details to your phone. Tatsu is filling up the gas tank as we speak. You and Reina can leave when you are ready. I've left instructions at the hotel concierge to charge the room and food expenses to my card. There is no need for either you or Reina to worry – especially about money."

"Brother, that's—" Hajime started.

Masashi knew his brother was going to argue, so he cut him off. "We do everything we can for family. Let me handle the logistics so you and Rei have less things to worry about. You just worry about driving to Tokyo safely. I'll receive no arguments, little brother."

"Masashi is right. Let Masashi worry about all the details for Tokyo and the rest of us with all the responsibilities here. You get yourself and Reina to Tokyo safely. Support her during this very difficult time," their eldest brother, Itsuki said.

CHAPTER 17

The atmosphere in the car was heavy. Hajime kept glancing at Reina, who'd been sitting quietly beside him. He could tell by her expression that she was lost in unpleasant thoughts too, not that he expected differently.

Hajime reached over the centre console and gently took her hand. He gave it a squeeze as he looked back towards the road. It was a smooth drive so far with hardly any traffic. A beat later, he felt Reina squeeze his hand back, their fingers lacing together.

"I'm not going to ask how you are or tell you it is going to be all right. But I'm here. If you want to talk, we'll talk. If you just want someone to listen, I'll listen."

Reina gave his hand another squeeze. "I know, Hajime. Thank you and…Happy New Year." A sad smile appeared on her lips.

Hajime looked at her before turning back on the road. He replied softly, "Happy New Year, Rei. I love you."

That stopped Reina's spinning thoughts. It was the first time she'd heard him say that. He usually just hinted at it, but never outright said it. She looked at him, and he gave her a soft smile.

"I love you too, Hajime." She was almost breathless. Without taking his eyes off the road, he lifted he brought their intertwined hands to his lips and placed a soft kiss over her knuckles.

***

As Hajime checked them in, Reina sent a message to her family, the Yoshidas, and her best friend to inform them that they'd arrived in Tokyo safely. She knew that her family and the Yoshidas were busy at the shrine greeting people for hatsumode. Her best friend probably wasn't awake, but she'd asked Reina to send word when they were in Tokyo.

To her surprise, Aika didn't reply but called her. "Rei, how are you? How are things?"

"I'm keeping it together. We are checking in at the hotel Masashi arranged for us. He did the impossible and got us a room. It looks like an expensive hotel but—"

"Let him take care of it. Knowing the Yoshida brothers, they consider you a sister—well, except Hajime. But seriously, it's Masashi's way of supporting you during this difficult time, so just accept gracefully."

Reina took a deep breath and exhaled. "You're right. I'll gracefully accept."

"Good. I'll let you go. I know it was a long trip. Rest if you can, okay?"

"I'll try. It's hard, but I'll try."

"Are you sure you don't need me there? I can drive over. I'm sure I can figure something out for lodgings."

"No, it's fine, Aika. I'll see you when we get back to Kyoto. Thank you, though."

"Okay. Call me if you need anything. I'll get there as soon as I can."

"Thanks, Aika. I will. You're the best." Hajime approached Reina just as she ended the call.

"Because of the holiday, they only have one room left—a last-minute cancellation." He explained.

Reina nodded. "Masashi is a miracle worker."

Hajime started laughing as he laid a hand on her lower back, guiding her to the elevators. "That he is."

When they got to their room, it was bigger both expected.

"Um, did they tell you at the concierge it was this big?" Reina asked.

"They did mention it being a junior suite, but it's more extravagant than I thought."

She looked up at him and commented, "I'm not sure how Masashi managed this but, I can't thank him enough."

Hajime wrapped an arm around Reina and said, "We will thank him together. For now, why don't you freshen up? There's still a few hours before the funeral parlour opens."

It was almost three in the morning when both of them were ready for bed.

There was only one bed, and Hajime insisted that Reina take it. She argued that she was smaller and would be more than comfortable sleeping on the couch. He wasn't hearing any of it though.

Reina then told him that she didn't think she could sleep. Now that they were settling down and had no distractions, her mother's death weighed on her mind. If she wasn't going to get any rest, she reasoned he should.

Without another word, Hajime took Reina's hand and pulled her towards the bed. He lifted the covers and coaxed her get under them, then lay on top of the covers beside her. He pulled her towards him and rest his chin atop her head as he cradled her in a gentle embrace.

"I'll stay until you're asleep," he whispered.

"Promise me, Hajime, no matter how I am received by Yuito's family and friends, please don't react."

"What do you mean? Did they hurt you when you were a child and living with your mom?" Hajime looked down at her.

Reina shook her head. "Mr. Suzuki...well...a few times...far in between...but he ignored me most of the time. As for his family... they didn't hurt me, but they were never...fond of me. I didn't really have any relationship with any of them."

Hajime nodded and gave her a squeeze. "Those are thoughts and discussions for later. For now, rest, my love."

***

Hajime sat beside Reina. He gritted his teeth. More than once, he had had to bite his tongue to keep from speaking. He had seen how the people around them had been treating Reina during her own mother's funeral. There were times when he heard whispers, backhanded comments. Reina would whisper to him who they were – either her stepfather's relative or friend. He noted thought that the people whom Reina pointed out as her mother's friends, never said anything negative to or about her.

The situation also showed him another side of Reina he'd never seen before. She could see and hear the exact same things he could, but her composure never wavered. She would keep her gaze fixed on her mother's picture while letting the people around her do as they pleased. She politely responded and bowed if someone talked with her or offered condolences. She never engaged in pointless squabbles or disrespected any of the people she knew had been saying bad things about her.

Hajime would hear things like, "Oh, that's the neglectful daughter! She never even bothered to visit her mother when she was alive. The nerve of her being here!" and "What is she doing here?" or "How did she even know? She hasn't been in contact with her mother for years!"

After lunch, Hajime quietly asked Reina, "Why do Mr. Suzuki's family and friends treat you with so much hate?" Your mom's friends seem to be all right with you."

Reina turned to him and answered, "I'm not really sure what he told them when I left Tokyo, but, when I lived with them, it was cold indifference at first. I thought it was because I am a daughter from a previous marriage. But then, Mr. Suzuki's sister married a man who had two children from a previous marriage, and he had custody over those children. I think it was because Mr. Suzuki hated me. I mean, I overheard one conversation he had with this brother-in-law about me. The brother-in-law noticed how Mr. Suzuki was treating me. Mr. Suzuki just told him that I was 'his wife's excess baggage'. He said I wasn't his daughter, so he had no obligation towards me whatsoever. But then, he did pay for my schooling so I think he and my mother had some words between them. He then told his brother-in-law I was a brat and often misbehaved, made his life miserable so at times, he had to 'discipline' me."

Hajime had to try very hard to school his reaction from one of disgust to a stoic calm.

"My mother eventually stopped bringing me to any Suzuki family functions, so I had very little interactions with them. Who knows what Mr. Suzuki had told them about me. My mom would tell me to hang out at a friend's house. I'd always wondered why. With an adult perspective, I suppose, or at least I choose to believe, it was my mother's way of getting me out of any kind of hostility."

Hajime took her hand into his and replied, "From what I can tell, it wasn't a big loss that you didn't establish any meaningful relationship with any member of Mr. Suzuki's extended family."

The rest of the day progressed in the same fashion as how things were during the morning. No matter what people said, grief was predominant on her features, something Reina couldn't mask. Hajime was both amazed and concerned for her. When they returned to their room after the wake, Reina let the grief flow out. Hajime silently held her, eventually convincing her to eat. After freshening up, he pulled her to the couch and simply held her. He wasn't sure how much time passed, but Reina fell asleep against him while he was brushing his fingers through her hair. Hajime then carried her to bed and tucked her in.

The funeral the following day was a repeat of the day before. The cremation was scheduled to happen at the end of the day. Hajime wondered about the smoothness of the whole thing; given that it was New Year's, shrines and temples were busy welcoming visitors for hatsumode.

The funeral parlour staff and Buddhist priest treated Reina as Reika's daughter no matter what protest came from her stepfather's family.

Around noon, they prepared for the cremation. A staff member ushered Reina her to where they were cremating her mother's body. While some of her stepfather's extended family members were quite vocal with her being there, the staff politely explained that Reika had left instructions when she prepared the funeral packages for her and her husband, and they were specifically for her only child, Reina.

This surprised Reina, but she remained silent. There would be time after all the proceedings to ask the staff exactly what her mother had prepared.

Hajime waited anxiously outside for Reina as the cremation started. He leaned against the wall in the hallway and straightened as soon as he saw Reina walking out. She looked distressed, so he took her hand in his own.

Before he could say anything, one of the staff members apologized for intruding and explained that he would call Reina when the cremation was over in a few hours. He directed them towards a waiting room.

A few hours later, when Reina stood beside the metal table with her mother's ashes, she was handed the long, metal chopsticks to move the bone fragments to the urn. She quietly finished the task, her hands shaking the whole time. The staff transferred the remaining ashes in the urn before sealing it.

Reina went through the motions when she was handed her mother's urn, then followed the Buddhist priest and the Suzuki family. It was all a blur.

When the urns were interred, the Suzuki family matriarch looked towards Reina and said, "You've done whatever it is you needed to do. You can leave now. You are not part of the Yuzuki family. Let my family grieve in peace."

Reina didn't expect that. She was startled and before she could react or reply, Hajime had stepped in front of her and said, "I understand you've just lost your son and daughter-in-law, but that doesn't excuse you for treating her like this. She lost her mother. You have no right to tell her not to grieve or deny her right to say goodbye."

The older woman looked like she was going to say something more, but her husband told her to stop.

Hajime felt Reina's hand against his back. He looked at her over his shoulder.

"Let's go, Hajime. I've said my goodbyes. I'm ready."

He gave a nod, and without another word, he turned to Reina and guided her back.

"You didn't have to leave," Hajime whispered as walked.

Reina shook her head. "No, it's really fine." She glanced up at him. "I want to talk with the funeral parlour staff. They made a comment inside the cremation room about how Mom had left instructions for me when she prepared the funeral packages. I want to know more about it."

CHAPTER 18

The parlour director welcomed Reina and Hajime at his office. "What can I do for you, Ms. Maruyama? I was told that you had some questions."

"Pardon us, Mr. Kikuchi. I was told earlier that my mother, Reika Suzuki, had made the preparations for everything herself?"

The man gave them a side smile before excusing himself. He got up and retrieved a folder. "Reika Suzuki came to us with a lawyer. They explained that they were preparing a will. She wanted the will to have a plan that included funeral arrangements. We talked about every single step. She gave instructions on which temple needed to be contacted for the religious rites and the financial coverage. We were also told that you are the most important person to be contacted—that you are her daughter, and she wanted you to be included in everything."

He handed Reina the folder, then excuse himself to give her time to read through all the documents.

"I don't understand," Reina commented after a while. A sharp pain pierced through her heart. Anger also ran through her veins. "Mom planned all this, made sure I was included in all of this, but she never told me anything. Why?" Exasperation. Grief. Confusion. Anger. Pain. Reina had to close her eyes and concentrate on her breathing to try and calm down. She stood and started pacing back and forth. Her mind wasn't working. She couldn't think of any plausible answer to '*why?*'

Hajime wondered himself.

Reina walked back towards the table and closed the folder, leaving it on the director's desk. She laid her hands on her lap, let out a breath, and turned to Hajime. A soft but sad smile appeared on her lips. "Let's go. I think we learned all we can. In a way, I'm relieved that Mom prepared for this, whatever her reason."

Hajime nodded as he offered his hand. "It could have been more stressful, especially for you, if she didn't do what she did. I'd like to believe she did it for you."

Reina wrapped her arms around his waist and nodded against his chest. Hajime squeezed her and stepped back as she stood to leave the office.

Outside, they thanked the director again. As they were leaving the building, a woman carrying a huge white box approached them.

Hajime stiffened, ready to block Reina from the woman's path. He had seen the woman during the wake and funeral with the people who'd been talking about his girlfriend. He didn't trust anyone associated with them.

The woman stopped walking when she noticed Hajime tense up. "I'm sorry." She bowed deeply and said, "Ms. Maruyama, do you remember me? I don't mean any harm."

Hajime decided to stay quiet, but he felt Reina shift.

The woman lifted the box she was holding. "Do you remember me, Rei? It's been years but I hope you somehow do recall me a bit. I was your mother's best friend."

Reina nodded and offered a weak smile. The woman slowly approached. When she was close enough, she offered the box to Reina. "Your mother wanted you to have this. She told me that if something ever happened to her, I was to give you this. She had always been proud of you. I always reprimanded her when she would receive something from you and wouldn't reply. I know it hurt when she abandoned you when you were younger, but please believe me when I say she did it out of love."

It overwhelmed Reina as the gravity of what her mother's best friend had revealed. She took the box. It felt heavier than it ought to have been. She cleared her throat before bowing. "It's nice to see you again, Mrs. Nishida. I'm sorry I didn't approach you earlier. This is my boyfriend, Hajime Yoshida. If it's okay…um…would it be all right if…I ask you about Mom?"

The older woman smiled. "Sure, and don't worry about it, dear. I would be honoured to answer any question you might have. Are you two returning to Kyoto right away? May I invite you to lunch tomorrow?"

"We can stay another day, Mrs. Nishida," Reina answered as Hajime nodded in agreement.

"I would have invited you for dinner, but she told me what's inside the box, and I anticipate you'll want some time to process the contents."

"Thank you, Mrs. Nishida." Reina bowed towards her again. Numbers were exchanged before the older woman parted ways with Reina and Hajime.

***

Upon arriving at the hotel, Reina laid the box on the coffee table and sat on the floor in front of it. Hajime gave her some space. He busied himself by the kitchenette, preparing some tea. As he poured water into the kettle, he heard Reina call for him.

He hurried to her side. Before he could ask anything, Reina looked at him and reached for his hand. She pulled him beside her.

On the table, he saw an open photo album and realised he was looking at a picture of a younger Reina.

"Hajime, this was during the first Gion festival I went to since returning to Kyoto. I'd recovered enough from my injuries, so my grandmother and your mother helped me choose a yukata for the festival. Tatsu and I went. I skimmed through the pages and the pictures… they're all there…all my milestones…graduations… sports days…festivals… my coming-of-age day…us together last Christmas. She watched me from afar. She never stopped loving me."

Tears ran from her eyes. Hajime wrapped an arm around her shoulder. "Of course, she didn't stop. She may have had her reasons when she took herself out of your life, but you never stopped being her daughter. She loved you enough to let you go and be happy again with family in Kyoto."

"Why didn't she ever answer?"

Hajime gave her shoulder another squeeze and dropped a kiss atop her head. He looked over at the box and saw another smaller box inside. He realised that Reika left her daughter far more than he and Reina expected. Reika had definitely been a planner.

He watched as Reina set aside the album and reached for the smaller box.

When Reina opened it, a gasp left her lips. It contained every single letter and greeting card she had sent her mother over the past years. All had been opened and looked to have been taken out often, some more often than the others based on the severity of the wear and tear of the papers. Stacks of envelopes had been tied together by a string—all letters addressed to Reina that had never been mailed. Alongside them, there were two sealed envelopes, separated from the others. One was addressed to her and the other was addressed to Reika's "son-in-law".

Reina and Hajime looked at each other for a long moment. She cleared her throat and kept the letter addressed to 'my son-in-law' for safe keeping. Reina didn't want to be presumptuous to guess it was for Hajime since no talks of marriage had been broached between the couple. Taking another deep breath for fortification, Reina opened the letter addressed to her.

CHAPTER 19

My Dearest Daughter,

Forgive your mother for being a coward. There is no excuse because I let my weaknesses colour my decisions. If you are reading this now, then the worst has happened, and I am no longer in this world. Asking for your forgiveness might be presumptuous of me and I will never blame you if you can't. That the is the bed I've made and the truth I've accepted.

I am penning this letter for you now because out all the people in this world, you deserve to learn the truth from me. To be honest, doing this was unthinkable. If someone were to ask me a year ago if I intended to reach out to my daughter, I would have said no. But my therapist helped me realise...this is important...not just for you...but for me as well. I have been trying to get better but it's still a long road for me. I have every intention to keep updating this letter every now and then, as a safety measure for you to have answers if I don't get the chance to see you and explain in person.

Where to start? There are so many things I want to say to you but now that I'm trying to write it all down...the words won't come. I'll do my best to cover everything: things you need to know and things I want you to know.

I'll start with one very important thing – I have always wanted you! I am an imperfect mother who perhaps shouldn't deserve that title, but you are my precious daughter and I never, never regretted having you. I let you go because you deserve a better life than what I can give. I understand if you won't believe me – and that's okay – but know that I have loved you the moment I knew you were growing inside of me.

I remember when your father and I learned we were having you. Oh, how excited we were! My mother, your grandmother, had several miscarriages before she had me, so I was really afraid to do something wrong and miscarry you. I followed every single one of my doctor's advice to make sure you grew healthy inside me. I will always be grateful for your grandmother, Yuzuki, and Mrs. Yoshida, Yuuka. They were patient with me, ready to answer my questions and reassure my fears.

What aggravated my fears was the fact that I was throwing up excessively. My doctor diagnosed me as having hyperemesis gravidarum. The term is scary enough by itself because we don't hear it often. It simply means severe nausea and vomiting that doesn't go away with some people until after pregnancy – I was one of those. I had to be hospitalised for several hours a number of times because of dehydration, except that one time where I lost too much weight and my doctor was concerned that it might affect you. I had to stay for three days because of it.

When you were born...when the nurse put you in my arms...you were perfect. Ten fingers. Ten toes. Very pink and crying. Healthy. The overwhelming love and relief were the things that rushed through me. Your father...my Yuuki cried. I'd never forget his face when he first held you. His eye reflected the love he had for you. It shown so brightly. When the tears of joy came, he didn't care who saw because we had just been given such a priceless treasure.

I wish I could tell you that it was completely perfect after. The throws of the afterbirth...my hormones levels were...I wasn't myself for a while. I couldn't break away from the tiredness...the anxiety...the extreme sadness...I felt like a failure because I couldn't even breastfeed you properly...I wasn't sleeping properly...at first, I thought it was normal because I was warned by a lot of ladies that you'll feel baby blues after giving birth. But when it was lasting more than two weeks, Yuuki insisted that I talk to a doctor about it. It was when I was diagnosed with postpartum depression. Yuuki became even more of my rock.

With medical help and your father's unwavering support, I got over my postpartum depression. Through it all, it was your father who stepped up to make sure my condition didn't affect you. He pleaded with me to use a breast pump because we were both informed that breastmilk was the best for you within your first year of life. He made sure I ate a well-balanced diet. Early in the morning, he would wake me up and force me to get up. We'd take a walk around the park.

Please don't forget the happy memories we've had when you were young and your father was still with us. My favourite memories were the ones where I'd come home and I saw you two in the kitchen, heads down and different bowls of dried tea leaves in front of you. I loved going to different restaurants, cafes, and kiosks to try different desserts. One of my favourite family trips was when we took you to Shizuoka to see the tea farms. Your father was in heaven seeing that. And so much like your daddy's, I've always treasured your expression of complete awe.

We were so happy…so…so happy…your father and I were even talking about having another baby. When you father was diagnosed…our world fell apart. The cancer was very aggressive. When his doctor gave us the news that he only had a few months to live, it made me angry when Yuuki decided not to have any treatment. I tried to talk him out of it. I tried to convince him to try, but he had been adamant and steadfast in his decision. He said he would rather spend the last of his days comfortable with family instead of being sequestered at the hospital. I didn't want to consider a world without Yuuki. I thought it was extremely unfair that a perfectly wonderful man, kind, generous, and always laughing, was dying. I started grieving even before he died.

I know it was selfish but…I couldn't stop the feeling of anger, sorrow, and anticipated loss. I already lost my mother. I lost her when I was your age. Watching her slowly wither away made me feel helpless and lost. It was your father who stood by me and kept me together while I was forced to learn quickly what it meant to plan for a funeral. But I would be alone in dealing with everything when he passed.

I knew Yuuki prepared a lot for his death. I was aware that he left all his instructions to your uncle instead of me – for which I wholeheartedly support and even admire. I would have made even more of a mess if your father left his instructions and things to pass on to you with me. When I noticed his journals and collections were gone from the house, I asked him if he forgot anything.

I think I surprised him because his eyes widened. I don't think he expected me to know and not say anything about it until after he had executed his plans. I watched your father's facial muscles tense before calming, leaving a serious expression that told me there was something else he wanted to do.

Reina, your father feared about what will happen to you after he passed, and he had every right to. He watched me fall apart and inconsolable when my mother died. He walked me through recovery from my postpartum depression. He was there for you when I needed the time to focus on recovering properly. Yuuki knew the high probability of what would happen to my mental state the moment he passed, and he feared the repercussions of my breakdown on you. He told me to allow you to live with his family until the time I could get myself together.

Logically at that time, I understood what your father was saying. I remember even feeling annoyed that he would think that…that he didn't trust me. Looking back now, Yuuki knew me far greater than I knew myself. For all the terrible things…the suffering that I let happen in your life…there are not enough words of apology to take it away…to make you forget. I am so, so sorry. Perhaps my words now are too late, but I hope they will finally help you heal.

What I am about to share with you now are things I don't normally talk about – not a lot of people know about them. These are things I have kept buried inside me and let fester until it became too big to contain and it hurt more than me. These won't justify my decisions and my actions. They will never erase the fact that I am responsible for you undergoing so much emotional abuse at such as tender age, after you had lost your beloved father.

Earlier in my letter, I revealed to you that your father and I contemplated on having another child. With your father's illness, the idea was naturally shelved. The cancer had been very aggressive. But shelved or not, it didn't matter because it was soon after the diagnosis… we found out that I was pregnant. During my annual check for work, my pregnancy was detected – six weeks. It was bittersweet. Don't misunderstand, Reina. Your father and I were thrilled to be having another child, but the ultrasound…the doctors gave us the devastating news that I had an ectopic pregnancy. The baby implanted outside of my womb…at one of my tubes…and there was no way to save the pregnancy. I had to have an emergency surgery.

He would have told you and the rest of the family, but I begged not to…not yet. I told him I wanted time to accept…to grieve in privacy. Bless that man. He simply nodded. In truth though, I wanted to concentrate on Yuuki's health instead. It seems illogical, I know, but at that time, it felt like it was the right decision. By not saying anything, it somehow felt like it wasn't as painful as it was. I was praying for a miracle that he will get well. It was never confirmed though I felt like we were going to have another baby girl. That's why we decided to give her the name, Akari, our bright light who was in heaven, watching over all of us. Now…I know I also did my youngest daughter harm by not acknowledging her properly. My only consolation now is that your father is with her. I'm sure he's taking good care of her.

I didn't realise that I was building a house of cards when I made the decision to hide my ectopic pregnancy and subsequent loss of a baby. I think Yuuki did. Because even though he respected my decision, he was straightforward in his instruction – give you to Ichigo and your grandparents when the time comes that I can't take care of you. Not 'if'… it was 'when'.

I did Yuuki, especially you, a disservice and irreparable hurt by refusing to acknowledge my incompetence for years. I kept telling myself I'm not a bad mother, and that things were simply out of my control. But that's the focal point of all the terrible things you went through…it was in my control…all of it. I kept reasoning that you already lost your father at such a young age, you didn't deserve to lose your mother too. You were all I had left of my Yuuki. I couldn't let you go.

I know you were angry at me when I wasn't at your father's bedside during his last hours. No reasoning will make it sound okay. I couldn't watch him die, Reina. It felt like I was dying with him. It felt like something was strangling my throat…I couldn't breathe. It felt like my heart was being pierced by needles consistently. When he passed, it felt like a part of me died with him. My memories after that were a blur. In the middle of my grief, I remembered I still had you.

I know how fragile life can be, so I'm sure by now you know what I've done to prepare for my eventual death. I don't know when I will be leaving this world, but when I do, I'll be sure to spare you the stress of worrying about my funeral, especially the money required to pay for it. I made you my emergency contact in the hopes that if something happens, you will be informed. You will not go through life guessing what happened, especially if I haven't reached out to you in person yet.

***

Reina closed her eyes as she set the letter down in front of her. While it was heartbreaking to read about the struggled her mother faced before Reina was even born, Reina couldn't help but agree with her mother when she called herself 'selfish'. Her mother *was* selfish. Indignant anger was suddenly overwhelming Reina's body. Her hands were shaking that she finally let go of her mother's letter.

Wanting to somehow distance herself from the letter, Reina stood up and walked towards the hotel window. Her jaw was clenched as she clutched her hands tightly. She forced herself to breathe deep.

The city of Tokyo was buzzling from beyond the window. There were a lot of people walking on the sidewalks below, different vehicles driving though, trains passing at regular intervals at a distance away. But Reina was seeing none of them. She was so lost in her mind that she didn't even notice Hajime approaching her from behind. She jumped as soon as Hajime's hands landed gently on her shoulders.

"I'm sorry for scaring you, love," his ran both of his thumbs on her shoulders as an apology, "I didn't realise you didn't hear me."

Reina shook her head before stepping back and leaning against him. Hajime automatically wrapped his arms around her. "It's fine, Hajime. I wasn't paying attention," she told him, allowing the comfort he offered to envelop and calm her.

"What happened? Are you okay?" He whispered.

Reina took a moment before answering you, "You asked me once...about the father's journals."

"Yes, I remember," he wanted to say more but he allowed her the silence to gather her thoughts.

"I gave you a general summary of what the contained. I never gave you any details."

"It wasn't really my business to know, Rei, so I didn't expect you to be specific," he looked down before continuing, "I am assuming your mother said something in her letters that your father also wrote about."

Reina sighed. It was all the acknowledgement Hajime needed. She turned around within his embrace and looked up. "In one of dad's journals...one of his last ones...he wrote about my sister," she felt him stiffen around her as she also watched his eyes grow wider, "My mom was pregnant when dad got sick. Both of my parents explained that it wasn't a viable pregnancy from the start."

"What do you mean?"

"My sister didn't settle in my mom's womb to grow. She grew outside of it. It was an ectopic pregnancy. Do you know what that is?" When Hajime shook his head no, Reina continued, "It happens when the fertilised egg implants itself anywhere but the womb. It is dangerous because there isn't space for the baby to grow so that kind of pregnancy is a medical emergency. The longer the baby grows, the higher the risk to the mother's health. There's no possible way to save the pregnancy."

Hajime to a moment to process what Reina had said. His heart clenched at the realisation of what she said meant. Tightening his embrace, he said, "I'm so, so sorry, love. She would have been just as beautiful as you."

"It would have been amazing growing up with a sister...and I do *have* a sister. She's just with our dad and perhaps it is a good thing. She never had to suffer in this world."

Hajime didn't know how to respond to that and so had let it go. He quickly reviewed what she said earlier and redirected the conversation. "Your father wrote about her on his journals?"

Reina broke from the embrace and gently took Hajime's hand, pulling him along towards the couch. "My sister's name is Akari. To be fair, no one was able to determine if the baby was a boy or girl but according to mom, she felt like it was a girl so she and dad named her Akari. Based on my mom's letter, she didn't know that dad *did* tell me...sure not verbally but he wrote it down in one of his journals. And that's what makes me angry... granted that dad was just diagnosed with cancer...he...Uncle Ichigo...my grandparents were already devastated...me. My mother decided to keep the truth about Akari between her and dad, saying that she wanted to grieve in private. I can understand wanting to grieve but what about the rest of us?"

Reina wiped the angry tears she started shedding. "Even in his most trying time, dad supported mom...respected her decision at the expense of himself. He was suffering, grieving for my sister alone, Hajime! Based on his journal entries, after the surgery, he and mom barely talked about it. He poured his grief on those pages. It makes me angry reading what my mom wrote but at the same time, I knew she was grieving too...it just annoys me that she writes about how dad supported *her,* but she hasn't intimated in the parts I have read *how she* supported my dad. She wrote how much she loved dad but...I guess...in the depths of my heart I didn't forgive her because...I suppose I was looking at proof that she did love dad... love us."

Hajime took out his handkerchief and started wiping at his girlfriend's tears.

"Why did I even come here? Maybe we...I shouldn't have come," Reina commented.

It sounded like a rhetorical question but Hajime chose to answer, "Closure. As frustrating, infuriating, and painful things are now, what comes after is closure. You won't have 'what ifs' or 'might have been'.

CHAPTER 20

Hajime laid a cup of tea in front of Reina before setting his on the coffee table. He settled beside her before he asked, "Do your grandparents and uncle know about Akari?"

Reina nodded before she took a sip. "After I finished reading dad's journals, I was so aghast that I ran to the kitchen. I probably should have been more conscientious in asking...I simply blurted it out... if they knew about Akari," she looked down as her face reddened. With a hint of shame in her voice, "My grandparents didn't know, love. They didn't know about her. Uncle Ichigo admitted that my dad told him about her but explained that dad had wanted to be the one to tell me and my grandparents. I did a bit of research... according to an ordinance from the Ministry of Health and Welfare, if the baby is less than four months, the parents have no obligation to notify the authorities about their child's death. If the child were twelve weeks or more, the child would be considered stillborn and the local government will need to receive a stillbirth notification form from the parents and the stillbirth certificate issued by a doctor or midwife. In both situations, the child will not be registered in the family register. My sister was only six weeks old. There's no record about her," Reina paused before a nostalgic look crossed her features, "After I explained what I've read from dad's journals, grandmother and I went out to buy a flower – the yume-akari rose. Grandmother said it was perfect – *yume* for a beautiful dream, and *akari* for the everlasting light. The flowers you've seen around my grandparents' house and the Maruyama family plot at the temple, they are yume-akari. She may not be officially registered in the family register, but she's still a Maruyama."

"That's a beautiful tribute, Reina. I'm sure Akari enjoys it from heaven."

"Dad and Akari are together," she paused as a thought passed her mind, "as for mom…"

Hajime understood her train of thought. Not wanting to say the wrong thing, he cleared his throat. "Are there other things from your mom's letter?"

"I haven't finished reading it," Reina admitted. "Would you… would you read it with me? The first part of it was already earth-shattering, I don't think I have the emotional courage to do it alone."

"You don't have to finish reading it today if you're not ready."

"No. I think I have to. When we leave Tokyo, I want no baggage. I want to leave everything negative behind. I'm not bringing this to my future…to our future."

Hajime moved closer to her and put an arm around her shoulder. He then reached over to the open letter. "Well, let's read this together. Where did you stop?"

***

I believe it is important for me to explain why I decided to move us to Tokyo. Rei, it was an opportunity I couldn't refuse. It was a promotion with higher pay. I truly thought it would be beneficial. A fresh start for you and me but as I'm sure you've come to learn, even if you leave a place, even if you run, inner demons don't leave you alone. To cope, I had been taking anti-depressants from the moment we lost your sister… more after your father. It worked for a while…for two years…and when you were eleven…it wasn't working anymore. I started mixing alcohol to my 'regimen'. I'm thankful enough that I had the presence of mind not to let you see. I always drank in my room, kept alcohol in my room. I drank more when you were in Kyoto for the long-school holidays.

My best friend, Marie, intervened. She didn't take no for an answer. She got me to the hospital at the start of your vacation and I started my rehabilitation. It helped me break the alcohol but not the pills. Since I had been doing it for years, it became like a safety blanket for me. I thought I couldn't function without pills. I figured since I was able to do my job…I was able to provide for you…send you to school…pay all our bills…able to function…it was okay. I told myself, I already sacrificed the alcohol, I wasn't going to give up another one that helps me function.

In one of the sessions, I received an advice about trying to move on and let your father go. In a moment of complete weakness, tired of always being in pain and always depressed, I turned my emotions to anger and redirected it to your father. Looking back now and talking with a professional, I realised that I also turned that anger towards you as your father's daughter.

That single decision led me to be receptive towards Yuito's suit. Yuito…I think he had always known that he chose a broken woman. I didn't love him at the beginning but the more we went out, the more my affection for him grew. I started feeling good again…to the point I actually gave up the pills so when you approached me to voice your concerns, I got extremely angry at you. I felt as if you were sabotaging my once chance to be happy again…that you wanted me in that perpetual darkness. It is unfair and completely unwarranted towards you. I am so, so sorry. My therapist explained that it was a defensive reaction for me because of a perceived threat towards me. He then went on to explain that while it is a defensive reaction, it doesn't make it right. You are my daughter. My instincts should have pushed me to nurture, not harm. It was explained to me that because I had been living in the bubble I created inside my head, I effective isolated myself mentally in an attempt to protect myself from all outside factors, including you.

I married Yuito even knowing your feelings. He loves me with all his heart, I know this. I was finally happy. I was no longer alone in dealing with life. I had support. But I haven't been able give him children... something he wants so much. The ectopic pregnancy left me practically barren. The doctors I went to for second-, third-, fourth opinions have all explained that because one of my fallopian tubes and ovary were removed, taking into account my age, it was next to impossible to conceive. I felt like a failure as a wife because I couldn't give my husband the children he wanted. I started the pills again. Yuito was aware. It was difficult for him to miss because my memory turned spotty and I would check out mentally, even though we would be in the middle of a conversation. I'm sure you remember just as you turned a teenager, a year into my new marriage, I lost my job.

I should have sent you to live in Kyoto when that happened but pride, no matter how false that pride was, dictated to by brain that I am your mother. I know what's best. I will not give you away and be a failure. How hypocritical of me. I failed you.

Yuito took over the financial aspect of our household. The private secondary school you went to was very expensive and he wanted to take you out of it, to go to a cheaper school but I told him he wasn't going to take you out of there. I think it was the only lucid thing I did...to put my foot down with regards to you. Your education was important. I wasn't going to compromise on that even with me borderline, losing my mind. It was non-negotiable. To pacify Yuito, I started part-time jobs to help with your tuition, club materials, and also...to fund my 'habit'.

I was so slow to realise that Yuito resented you because of money. He was paying for you – someone whom he considered not his daughter – to go to school, to keep you healthy, and he couldn't have kids of his own. He took out his frustrations on you. When I saw him hit you one time – yes, I saw when you both didn't know I had come home early and with the door open to the kitchen – I told him I'd divorce him for hitting you. I think that was the last time he physically hurt you. He apologised and said he wouldn't hurt you anymore. I believed him. He started avoiding you. He paid for everything you needed without complaint. But I do understand that it will never excuse his earlier behaviour.

On the day of the accident, I heard you call when you arrived. I was at the downstairs toilet. I had exited and at the bottom of the stairs intending to follow you up to talk with you about the school trip fees I was going to ask you to pay the following day. I saw Yuito storm out of our bedroom and bumped into you. I screamed on reflex. He tried to grab you but missed. I tried to catch you but with the configuration of our staircase, I was only able to clear the lower steps before it turned at an angle to the steps that led upstairs.

I panicked. I wanted to pick up, get you out of there but it was Yuito who said not to touch you because we didn't know how you were injured. He said that we might injure your neck. He called for emergency services. Your accident still causes me nightmares until now. It is one of the most horrifying things I've ever seen.

I couldn't deny reality much longer. I couldn't save you too…I failed as your mother. I should have listened to your father and admitted I need a lot of help…that I was not okay.

It was then I knew I had to let you go. I contacted your uncle and told him what happened. I asked him to get you. Not simply visit, but to get you. He came to Tokyo right away. The very next day I got a lawyer to process my surrendering of parental rights to your uncle. It was very difficult to give you up, but I did it. I wanted you to have a clean break from me to heal…to blossom to be the wonderful lady you've turned out to be.

But I forgot one very important thing. I forgot you are my Yuuki's daughter. I broke down when I received the first card from you. Every time I receive something from you, it makes my resolve to stay out of your life harder, but my shame of being a 'failed mother' would come.

My maladaptive behaviours made me ill-equipped to raise you. Pills. Alcohol. Inner demons. All of it made me feel unworthy to be your mother. I watched you flourish from afar. Knowing you are happy and excelling strengthens my resolve that I actually made the right decision for you.

Don't hate your uncle, but he kept me appraised about you for years. He knew the disappointment you felt every time you tried to reach out to me. He had been trying to convince me to reach out to you but I'm a coward. I always told him that I will when I got better. I kept saying 'when I will be…' that I didn't notice that the years passed quickly. When I realised that you were graduating university, I became proactive and sought professional help – thus this letter. It has helped banish some of my demons but there are a lot more.

For now, I satisfy myself into believing that you are flourishing. I watched you bloom into the wonderful lady you are now. You're about to finish university, and I couldn't be prouder.

In the box, you will find a white silk kimono. This wedding kimono has been passed down on my side of the family for generations. It has always been given to the eldest daughter. I wore it when I married your father. You don't need to wear it for your own wedding, but I'd like you to have this heirloom.

You'll also see a small jewellery box. I am leaving you the necklace your father gave me when you were born. You might remember me wearing it a lot all those years ago. It has the sunflower charm that you loved to play with whenever I carried you when you were a baby.

I still sparingly wore it after your father died. I never told Yuito it was from your father. I spared him that heartache, but he does know that I got the necklace when you were born. It reminds me so much of you. He never said anything about that.

I don't remember much of the frantic moments of getting you to the hospital and waiting for the doctors to say that you were going to be okay. Yuito stayed with me at the hospital. He left when your uncle arrived.

I will forever be grateful to your uncle and your grandparents for taking you in and raising you just like Yuuki would have wanted. They gave you the home that I failed to give you after your father's death.

Speaking of Ichigo, your uncle also told me about Hajime Yoshida. He told me that you are in a relationship together.

Reina and Hajime shared a look as the paused reading. A blush bloomed on Reina's cheeks. It never occurred to her that her mother would have been told about her relationship with Hajime. There was a page left to her letter. Reina wondered what her mother would be saying, especially about Hajime.

Hajime laid a sweet kiss on Reina's forehead before they started reading again.

***

All of us who have seen you two since you were babies aren't surprised. You two have always had a special bond. Cherish that. It is something very rare in this world.

If you two decide to get married, know that you have my blessing. I couldn't have picked a better son-in-law. It might be too early for me to say this, but like I said, you two have always had a truly special bond.

When you were learning how to walk, your first steps were towards Hajime. He had been watching over you for me while I prepared snacks with Yuuka. He called out to tell us you were walking. Out of all the people you chose to walk your first steps towards, you chose Hajime. You chose wonderfully, my Rei.

Hajime had always treated you with kindness. But most importantly, ever since you were children, he has always allowed you to explore and learn. He didn't always catch you because he wanted you to learn to get up by yourself. When you'd trip and fall as all babies learning to walk do, he encouraged you to try again. If it were to really hurt you, he was very quick to block you with his body so you wouldn't hit your head. He was only a baby himself. At five to six years old, he had already been really protective of you. We speculated it was because Yuuka was pregnant at the time. She said Hajime was excited to be a big brother for the first time instead of being the baby.

But years have passed, and looking back, I believe you two knew before anyone else that you belonged together. You both just had to grow up first.

Now, I am so happy for the both of you for finding a way back to each other. If you do get married, remember that you must choose each other every moment. It is all about respecting each other and making the conscious effort of choose each other and your family. Love is wonderful, l but sometimes, it gets forgotten when tempers flare.

Stand by him just like I know he will stand by you during the ups and downs of life.

Continue to live, Rei. If you have baggage from the past, I'm so sorry, but please let it go. Don't let it colour your future. You'll never forget, but please forgive me.

Let me replace the pain with love. It might be too much to ask, but believe that I love you. I'm sorry if I made you believe otherwise, but you are my daughter. I will always love you. I will always be proud of you.

Be happy, Rei. Choose to be happy…to love. You have such a big heart. Choose to fill it with love.

I know it's a lot to ask, but don't grieve for me too much. The pain of loss will never leave, but I am confident, especially with Hajime by your side, that you'll learn how to live with it. I wish I could have spared you more pain. Cry and then let me go. Live. Be happy. Love.

With all my love,

Mom

***

Reina broke down as soon as they finished reading her mother's letter. Hajime could only gather her in his arms and let her grieve. Her sobs were agonizing, gut-wrenching to hear. If he could take the pain upon himself, he would have done it in a heartbeat. He couldn't imagine what it felt like to lose a parent, let alone both at such a young age.

Life gave her so much struggle. It could break just about anyone, but he would make sure she was okay. He gave her a silent promise that he would weather this latest storm with her.

CHAPTER 21

"Let me take you out for dinner," Hajime whispered after Reina's tears had subsided. She looked up at him and he gave her a gentle smile. "There are a lot of things that you need to process. That won't happen tonight. I think it's best if we go out, enjoy Tokyo, and take your mind off things."

After thinking about it, Reina nodded. "All right. I've never really been around this area, so I wouldn't mind exploring with you."

Another smile spread across Hajime's lips. "I'd like that. There's so much here we can check out."

She offered a tiny smile in turn. "Um, tomorrow…before lunch with Mrs. Nishida…would you…um…would you like to see where I attended primary school and secondary school?"

"Now that's something I'd really like to see. But for now, why don't you freshen up and change out of your funeral kimono? I'll let Masashi and the others know that after lunch tomorrow, we'll be heading home."

***

Hajime led Reina towards a sushi restaurant. Reina's eyes were still a little puffy from crying, but she was staying strong. Hajime knew that Reina loved sashimi and would often order it when they went out together. He also knew that shrimp tempura was her comfort food. While she was in the shower, he did a quick check and found a restaurant near their hotel.

Reina reached for his hand as they left their hotel room.

"I keep thinking about what my mother said. Mom said that when I was learning how to walk, you were the person I took my first steps towards." Hajime squeezed her hand in response. "Thank you for always taking my hand no matter if things are calm or crazy."

"Thank you for trusting me." He didn't remember it, but it meant a lot to know they'd had a connection for so long. "You know, I have this distinct memory of your mom." Hajime exchanged glances with her before continuing, "It was summer. Dad was busy preparing for nagoshi no harae. Both your dad and uncle were helping the preparations for the mid-year cleansing ceremony. Mom had gone out to buy some things, so your mom was watching over you and Tatsu while she was also busy in the kitchen. Itsuki, Masashi, and I were doing some chores to help out."

"It was a normal day. After lunch, you and Tatsu took your usual naps. But then, you started to have a fever. Your mom wanted to bring you home, but mine hadn't arrived yet. She couldn't leave Tatsu alone. But then, Tatsu woke up and also started complaining of not feeling well. Your mom was almost in a panic. Taking care of two small sick children is, I understand, overwhelming. I remember Mom being especially stressed if more than one of us got sick."

"Anyway, you were asking for Kuma-san. You wanted Kuma-san but of course, since you were at my house, you didn't have your favourite stuffed bear. You were starting to tear up, so your mom asked me to come and sit. She asked if I'd be okay to help watch the two of you while she made porridge. Your little hand reached out to me. I even remember what you said. "Hajime, Kuma-san is not here. I feel bad." I patted your head and said, "I know you feel bad, little one. Tatsu is also feeling sick. Will it be okay if I hug you for Kuma-san instead?" When you nodded, I wrapped you in a blanket and sat you in my lap. You fell asleep not long after."

"Your mom came back. I remember her smile. The memory stood out because she'd asked me, "Will you watch out for Rei when you're both older?" I answered *yes* without any reservations. She gave me a mother's smile, full of relief. "You are a good boy, Hajime. You've always been special to Rei.""

Reina couldn't remember any of this, but she was glad he'd shared it with her. "I remember Kuma-san. I wish I still had it, but Kuma-san got lost when we moved to Tokyo. I kind of just hug the graduation bear you gave me now." Reina blushed with her admission.

Hajime smiled. "I'm happy that you love the bear. You haven't named it?"

Reina shook her head.

"That's fine," Hajime assured her with a laugh.

"Are we close to the restaurant?" When Hajime nodded, Reina added, "It seems we are close to a mall. If it's open, do you mind if we go walking around after dinner? Maybe we could find some souvenirs for our families, especially for Masashi."

"I was thinking of red wine, plum wine, or even sake. I think Masashi would like something like that."

"That's a good idea. Are we going for snacks or non-food souvenirs for our families?"

As they reached the restaurant, Hajime tapped on the touch screen to get their table assignment. "We can check it out and decide which is more appealing."

Once they reached the table, Hajime handed the tablet to Reina so she could order her choices first, then handed tablet back so Hajime could put in his order too.

While they waited, Reina said quietly, "I'm a little scared about tomorrow."

"If you're not ready to talk with Mrs. Nishida, I think she'll understand. You don't have to force yourself if it's too much."

Reina took a deep breath and leaned back on her seat. She closed her eyes and answered, "I don't know. After reading Mom's letter…

it's too much to process. I have a lot of questions, but it feels like I don't know how to ask them. At the same time, it's an opportunity I don't want to pass up."

Hajime reached across the table and took a hand. "She did say that she was supposed to invite us for dinner but she knew you'd be overwhelmed. I really think she'll be okay if you are not ready to talk with her. Don't force yourself, Rei. You just lost your mother. Her actions, plans, and all the things she left you changed so much for you. It's absolutely all right not to be ready."

A few stray tears slipped free, and Hajime squeeze her hand. Reina quickly wiped them away and took another deep breath to calm herself.

"Will you excuse me for a while? I'll just call her," she asked.

With Hajime's encouraging smile and nod, Reina stood and walked near the entrance. Their food started arriving. Hajime smiled when he saw what she'd ordered, especially the tempura. He arranged the dishes on her side of the table and prepared soy sauce with a little wasabi.

When Reina came back, she looked a little relieved. "How was it?" He asked.

"You were right. She understood. She just told me that I could message her or call her any time. She also said that when I was ready to ask about Mom, she would be willing to answer any questions I might have the best she could."

Hajime reach across the table and gave her hand a squeeze. "When you are ready, I'm sure it will be easier to ask the questions burning in your head. In the meantime," he gave her a playful smile, hoping to life her mood, "By the way I'm still looking forward to seeing where you attended school here in Tokyo."

Reina laughed before taking a bite of her tempura. Hajime silently congratulated himself for that small laugh. It was such a sweet sound. As he watched her eyes fill with delight from a simple tempura, Hajime silently considered it a small win. After the day she'd had, he was glad to have these small victories with her.

***

In front of a primary school, Reina didn't want to enter the gates. Instead, she led Hajime to a nearby park and sat in one of the swings.

"I didn't enjoy my last years of primary school. I never told anyone even when I visited Kyoto. I was bullied."

"What?!"

Reina didn't say anything right away. She started swinging. "My classmates made fun of my accent. Kansai accent. I never thought about it back home, but here, away from everything and everyone I love, it made me so different. It was hard. I missed Dad, you, everybody. I missed my life in Kyoto. I didn't want to leave Kyoto after all the holidays because I didn't want to go back to school. But seeing Mom working long hours, hardly ever home…I figured I needed to do well in school, so she doesn't have more problems. I promised Dad I'd be good for Mom. So…I kept my head down, studied hard and learned about accents and language."

"Because of that, I was able to enter a really nice secondary school. I also develop a deep fascination for our language, how words, accents, and literature affect our lives…how it weaves our past to the present and to our eventual future. I started enjoying secondary school…joined the volleyball club…made friends…I didn't use my Kansai accent…stayed busy with school more and more so I didn't have to return to a cold home. When the accident happened, I was confused. I got angry because I just couldn't understand, but I was also so happy to finally go home. Kyoto saved my life. It will forever be home."

There was silence between them as Hajime processed the details of Reina's life. She'd only briefly talked about her experiences before—never in this much depth.

"I'm sorry you felt alone at such a young age, Rei."

Reina jumped from her swing and clasped her hands behind her back. She bent to level her eyes with Hajime's and gave him a reassuring smile.

"I choose to believe it made me stronger. I learned the importance of the quiet…of hard work…of faith…of home. It brought me back to you, didn't it?"

Hajime gently cupped the back of back of her neck, then leaned forward and kissed her.

"Well then," he said as he pulled back, "since you liked your secondary school here, will you show me?"

"Of course," Reina pulled him up and started to lead him.

CHAPTER 22

Not long after returning to Kyoto, Reina sat next to Ichigo sharing a pot of tea at the Maruyama ancestral house's garden. Ichigo had just finished telling her about his communication with her mother over the years.

"Uncle," Reina started, "do you think my dad and Akari welcomed mom in heaven? Do you think...she's even in heaven?"

Ichigo looked at his niece. Her eyes were pensive but open. "Rei, in no way was your mother perfect, neither was your dad...you or me. Your mother's actions surely will be taken into consideration where she went after death. Her heart is also an important thing to consider...what she believed. All of us will be judged the same. As for your dad and sister, Yuuki was a fair man, who loved freely and took great care of the people he loved. Things in heaven are completely different from things here. I'd like to believe there is no isolation in heaven, only acceptance, peace, and love."

In the calm serenity of the garden of the Maruyama house around them, Reina allowed herself to reflect on her uncle's answer. She had witnessed her uncle infuriated on her behalf through the years when Reika, her mother, failed to answer Reina. At the same time, it was her uncle who had patiently sat with her through the years to listen to all the woes, confusions and questions she had. He always helped her process things and come up with her own realisations.

"It will take time for me to fully process what I've learned about my mom's life. She did admit she had more demons. I won't deny that some of things she said got me angry, especially on my dad's behalf...our family...but...you're right, Uncle Ichigo, she wasn't perfect. She did what she could, faulty as it often was."

"Take all the time you need, Rei," Ichigo looked down, his hand unconsciously clenched his cup of tea. It frustrated him to thinking about the lost opportunities both mother and daughter could have enjoyed together. He, himself, had to settle the anger he had towards his former sister-in-law but, he was immensely thankful towards her for Reina. She sent Reina to Kyoto back to family who could love her and nurture her as Reina deserved. "Reika knew you loved her, Rei. The mere fact that you never gave up on her was something she cherished very much. She was very, very proud of who you blossomed into. She was especially proud when you took over Amai Omoide when I was in hospital. She said it didn't surprise her at all. You are your father's daughter."

Reina stayed silent as she looked out towards her grandmother's garden. "I miss dad...is it bad that I miss him more than I miss my mom?"

"No, Rei. Having experienced what you did when you were with your mother in Tokyo, learning all the things you've only been recently been told about...having to change or broaden your perception of things you went through...those are a lot to process. You haven't settled your feelings and thoughts about those. Your feelings towards your mom may change in the future, or not, but never think you are a bad person for missing your dad more." Ichigo remembered the day his brother died. He had gone back to Amai Omoide to make sure things were in order before heading back to the hospital. He would forever regret leaving the hospital, even if it were only for an hour.

When he arrived, his parents had arrived at the same time with dinner at hand. His sister-in-law had also met up with them at the lobby. When they entered the room, they saw Reina on bed asleep beside her dad. With Yuuki's arm around his daughter, the pair simply looked asleep but as Ichigo walked towards the bed, his heart dropped to his stomach as an insurmountable grief coursed through his entire being.

Yuuki had passed away quietly. Ichigo's heart broke for the little girl his younger brother loved so much, looking so peaceful in sleep beside her father. His parents, Yuzuki and Kouji, as well as his sister-in-law, Reika, all saw the same thing he did. They all looked at each other, not knowing what to do. Eventually, Reika walked over to her daughter and gently rubbed her back to wake up Reina.

The little girl's eyes blinked open, confused on what was going on. "Mom...?" Reika's face crumbled and started crying. Reina sat up and tried to pacify her mother but then noticed that her grandmother also sobbing in her grandfather's arms. She saw the anguish on her grandfather's face as well. Ichigo could never forget the look of panic in Reina's eyes when she sought his eyes.

Reika had been so overwhelmed that Ichigo had decided to step forward. "Reina, sweetie...please come here," extending a hand to encourage her to approach him.

Reina shook her head and looked back at her dad. "Daddy?" she called out. "Daddy?" she started shaking him. "Daddy?!" Reina started to panic as Yuuki never reacted.

It was then that Ichigo steeled his spine and as gently as he could, grabbed Reina and pulled her away from Yuuki.

Reina's screams of, "No! Daddy! Daddy! I want my Daddy!" still haunt Ichigo's dreams. He knew, especially in the darkness of night when he was alone in bed and nothing proving to be a distraction, Ichigo would hear those screams – anguished-filled screams of his niece – for the rest of his life.

Looking at Reina at that moment, Ichigo cannot deny that his niece had experienced a lot in her young life. Ichigo laid a hand on his niece's shoulder, "I miss your dad too. I miss him every day. But I think he misses us too. We will see him again someday. In the meantime, let's work hard to make him proud while we are still here."

A smile graced Reina's lips as she looked up at the man, whom she was extremely lucky to have as an uncle, "Yes, let's do our best! That's why you have to be 100% healthy again!"

Ichigo grinned. He then reached over and ruffed Reina's hair, causing laughter to erupt from the both of them.

***

The four Yoshida brothers had agreed to visit a bar together. Since Tatsunori was a few months shy of twenty, he wasn't allowed to drink anything alcoholic. It was the first time all four brothers could go together.

Itsuki laid his glass on the table. He looked at Hajime, who was seated in front of him. "So, whatever is happening with the cases you're facing in France?"

"I'll have to head to France soon for the criminal case. Alexandre had settled the defamation of character and illegal termination already. He'd deposited the settlement money to my account in France."

"Are you planning to go alone or bring Rei along?" Itsuki asked.

"It depends on when Alexandre advises me to go. She has a few months of school left before graduation. Reina has finished all of the major things she needed to. I don't want to take her away from school and her graduation ceremony. She worked hard for her degree. But, if the schedule I'm given is after Rei's graduation, I'll ask her if she wants to come or not."

Tatsunori raised an eyebrow at his older brother. "You do know that she will say yes, right? The moment you tell her that it's for a hearing, she'd even insist." The rest of his brothers laughed and agreed to his comment.

"That's true. I was actually considering, regardless of when the hearing is scheduled, I'd like to take Rei to France after graduation as a sort of graduation trip," Hajime admitted.

All three of his brothers perked up interest. "I'm liking that idea. I've been trying to figure out what to give her as a graduation present. If you're sure about your plans, let me know. The plane ticket will be my gift," Masashi immediately offered.

"That's a good gift," Itsuki commented, "I'm actually thinking something different." All three of his brothers shifted their gazes to him. "I had started an investment portfolio for all three of you. There's this new program – which by the way I'd also like to get all you all started on that too – anyway, the new program encourages individual savings and investment in Japan. The profits from this program are exempt from capital gain tax. I've been preparing the amount – around 10,000 - to start her off. I'll be talking with her on further investment plans and management. Speaking of, I'll need to sit down with each one of you to talk about your accounts."

"The contract of my part-time job is ending soon, at the end of the schoolyear actually. I've been planning to look for another one but school had been extra busy lately. Between assignments, reports, exams, and finishing off the rest of my contract, I haven't been able to look and apply. I might have to pause any monthly top-up to my investments," Tatsunori revealed to his eldest brother.

Itsuki nodded in understanding. "That's not a problem, Tatsu. That's why I set you up with top-ups because I anticipated these irregularities. Focus on your schoolwork. There isn't any deficit on any of your accounts so you're fine."

"I'm free this weekend so just let me know when you'd want to meet," Masashi addressed his oldest brother.

"Saturday morning would be great, if you're okay. I'll even treat you to lunch,"

"Right! Saturday morning it is!" Masashi confirmed.

Itsuki sobered a little before asking, "Speaking of Rei, how is she doing? Really?"

Hajime exhaled loudly. "She's…coping."

"And how are you doing?" Masashi followed up. He had faith that his brother was strong—strong enough to support Reina properly, but even Hajime could get emotionally worn down. He had his own problems that were also heavy. "Don't say you're okay if you're not. We are brothers here."

"There are times when I catch myself doubting if I'm doing enough to support Rei. Then, I'm quick to reprimand myself for doubting."

Itsuki clicked his glass with Hajime's. "You two know that the rest of us are here for you two." Masashi then clicked his glass with Hajime's, followed by Tatsunori.

Hajime gave a nod. He raised his glass and simply said, "To family," to which his brothers repeated as they shared a drink.

"Speaking of family, Itsuki. Not to pry or anything, but I've noticed you and Haruka looking a little glum sometimes, especially around children," Hajime commented.

"I've noticed that too," Masahi echoed while Tatsunori nodded.

Itsuki sighed. He should have known that his brothers would notice. There was something difficult going on that neither he nor Haruka had shared with the rest of the family. Now that they were on to him, he'd have no choice but to fess up.

"About that…" he began, then took a sip of liquid courage. It was going to be a long night.

CHAPTER 23

It was graduation. The moment Reina accepted her diploma, a deep sense of accomplishment swept over her. She had worked so, so hard for this. After the ceremony, she met up with Aika. The two best friends hugged and congratulated each other It was a new start for the both of them. Aika took a job in Nara so they wouldn't be able to see each other every day, but it was only a brief train ride away, so it wasn't too bad,

Congratulations were exchanged with their other friends and classmates. It was not long before Hajime and Tatsunori walked up to them. Tatsunori gave them each a small bouquet of pink and purple peonies. Hajime gave Reina a bouquet of different coloured irises, lilies and roses and offered a smaller bouquet of yellow daffodils to Aika. Pictures were taken, and as the day was celebrated between friends and family.

"Would you like to come to lunch with us?" Hajime asked Aika.

"No, but thank you, Hajime. My mom, sister and little niece are here somewhere."

Hajime nodded in understanding. He had come to understand why she was Reina's best friend. Aika was supportive, loyal, and protective, and her feisty and outgoing personality complimented Reina's shyer and calmer temperament. Reina, Aika, and Tatsunori had even relayed stories about the three of them getting all sorts of adventures before Hajime had returned from France. That had been an afternoon full of laughs and teasing.

"I'll still see you before you move to Nara, right?" Reina asked.

Aika wrapped an arm around her shoulder. "Of course, Rei. By the way, are you free tomorrow? It's a girls' day out. Spa. Shopping. Food. There's this cafe my sister wants to try."

"Yeah, sure. Just let me know what time and where I'll meet you. A girls' day out sounds nice."

"Perfect! Oh, and it's my mom and sister's graduation gift to the both of us. They told me to invite you before we left the house this morning. So, we will see you tomorrow." With another hug, Aika excused herself to look for her family.

Hajime and Tatsunori stood on either side of Reina as they bid Aika farewell.

"We better be going as well." Hajime said as he rested a hand on the small of Reina's back.

"Itsuki is on his way. Dad and Mom have picked up your grandparents and uncle. Unfortunately, Haruka couldn't get away from work, and Masashi is on a business trip," Tatsunori explained.

"Masashi called me last night. He said he'd treat me to any restaurant I like when he comes back, but I asked him for a book instead," said Reina.

Both Hajime and Tatsunori laughed.

"That is so like you to ask for a book instead." Hajime commented.

"Hey! It's a compromise! He only has to get me a book if he has a chance to buy it. If not, I'll take the restaurant offer instead," Reina hurried to explain herself.

Tatsunori was still laughing as he said, "He'll probably get you the book you asked for and more. Masashi has always given you more than any one of us, his own brothers."

"Every time Masashi got frustrated with us because we were so rowdy, he said he wished he had little sisters instead," Hajime recounted fondly.

"You two are being ridiculous. Masashi would often treat all of us to ice cream, not just me."

The two brothers smiled. It did happen that way all the time. Masashi would get frustrated with his rowdy younger brothers, but once they'd calmed down, he'd treat them all to ice cream.

"Masashi, I think, has always been the most generous out of all of us," Tatsunori commented.

"Agreed. Itsuki took his position as the firstborn seriously and served as all our protector," Hajime started, and Tatsunori finished, "You were always helping mom in the kitchen so I don't it surprised anybody when you decided to go into the culinary arts. As for me…hmmm…"

"Well, I think you're the voice of reason. You have this ability to keep people level-headed. You're the sounding board for all your brothers," Reina commented.

At that, both Hajime and Tatsunori nodded in agreement. Hajime shared a look with Tatsunori and gave a subtle nod, signalling that it was time. His brother gave a small, acknowledging nod.

"Here, let me carry your flowers for you. I'll head over to the restaurant first. Why don't you and Hajime take your time?" Without another word, Tatsunori gathered Reina's bouquets and walked away.

Reina was startled by the suddenness in the suggestion. She looked up at Hajime, who simply smiled and took her hand to lead her through a small park. "I thought we were in a hurry?"

"This path also leads to the restaurant. We are just taking a longer route," Hajime explained.

It was a very peaceful walk. There were hardly any people at the park. Considering it was a weekday afternoon, it was understandably empty.

Hajime sat them down at a bench near the pond. Reina looked at him curiously but said nothing.

Hajime took a deep breath. "Alexandre called and said I need to travel to France to testify in court."

"All right. When do you need to leave?"

"Next week." He then turned to her and added, "I'd like for you to come with me."

"Of course! I'll go with you."

Hajime ran this thumb atop her hand and smiled. "I also would like to show you where I studied, places I often visited, and the people who became like family to me. I want to share that part of my life with you just like what you did with me in Tokyo."

Reina squeezed his hand and smiled. "I'd love that."

But then Hajime did something she wasn't expecting so soon. He suddenly knelt on one knee beside her. "We've known each other for our entire lives. I've known you since you were in your mom's womb. While we've only been in a romantic relationship for about a year, I know you're the one for me. It was always you, Reina."

He looked into her eyes as he took a deep breath to calm his nerves. Then, he asked her the question that would change both their lives forever. "Will you marry me?"

Tears pricked Reina's eyes as she lifted a hand and cupped his cheek. "Yes."

Hajime leaned forward as she met him to share their first kiss as an engaged couple. Smiling, he gently took her left hand and slid a diamond ring on her finger. He quietly exhaled, relieved that he'd gotten her ring size right.

"I love you," Reina said.

Hajime stole a small kiss and replied, "I love you too." He stood and gently pulled her up. "Let's go. Our families are waiting."

Arriving at the restaurant, the waitress led them to the private room where everyone was waiting.

Greetings and congratulations were exchanged, and just before Reina and Hajime sat down, they looked at each other and smiled. Turning to their families, Reina lifted her left hand to show her ring.

An excited gasp filled the air as another round of congratulations came up, and embraces, celebratory pats, and tears of joy were exchanged.

Itsuki gave his younger brother a warm hug and whispered, "I am thrilled for you, Brother. You both deserve to be happy."

***

That evening, Hajime accompanied Reina home. After checking for tickets to France, they booked their flight, reserved their hotel room, and planned out their trip. It got complicated when they had to figure out the financial aspect of the trip.

Masashi had paid for Reina's tickets as his graduation gift. Reina was adamant that she paid half for their accommodations and food budget. Hajime was resistant at first but Reina was quick to remind him that she had been a paid worker of Amai Omoide from the moment she turned into an adult.

While she was the next generation Maruyama heir and part of the property and business were already under her name thanks to her father, Reina worked hard and saved most of what she earned. Aside from her basic, every day necessities and treats to herself every now and then, Reina didn't have a habit of splurging. She argued that she could afford her half of the trip. Hajime conceded and that settled the argument.

After all was said and done, they put on a movie and relaxed next to each other on the couch.

"Thank you for my amazing graduation present," Reina whispered as she looked up at Hajime.

His arm wound around her in a tight embrace before he planted a kiss on her forehead. "I actually haven't given you your gift yet."

"What do you mean? We got engaged today. You're sharing your life in France with me. Basically, you welcomed me into your life even more."

Hajime's eyes softened. "Don't get me wrong, but those are pretty much gifts for me too. I actually have another one, specifically for you. Remember when we talked about you being concerned with your English skills a couple of months ago?"

"Yes."

"I bought a subscription for you. It's an online program where you choose your schedule. You can try a group class or a one-on-one class. It's billed monthly, so if you feel confident enough, you can stop it at any time. Offline, I'll be your language partner."

Reina's jaw dropped. "Hajime, it might get expensive—"

"It is a priceless investment, and it's something I know you wanted. Don't think of the money. Concentrate on reaching your goals. Besides, if we work together and we both become fluent, it will help us with our special work project. Always remember, though, that I will never regret investing in you."

Reina wrapped her arms around his neck. She whispered, "You are so amazing. I'm so blessed to have you and your love."

Hajime hugged her closer and buried his face in her hair. He loved her, but more than that, he'd found his perfect partner. He knew they would fight together through any challenge. There was no doubt in his mind that they would choose each other no matter what life threw at them—the good times and the bad.

After settling back to continue their movie, Reina's phone chimed with a new message. She reached for her phone on the coffee table and read Haruka's congratulatory message, then shot back a quick reply before leaning back.

"Hajime, is something going on with Haruka and Itsuki? I know it's not any of our business, but lately I've noticed that something is…wrong…or bothering them…I can't really explain it."

Hajime sighed. "So, you've noticed it too…"

In a soft voice, Reina answered, "It's difficult not too…"

"At the point, we can only hope they'll figure it out and things will turn out better for the both of them."

CHAPTER 24

Raphael had been the one to welcome Hajime and Reina to France. Hajime was both nervous and excited to be back. He wanted his legal situation over so he could finally completely move on with his future with Reina. For her part, Reina was excited to visit France for the first time but also nervous for Hajime. She knew the stress of the testifying was weighing heavily on him. Plus, it was his first time back to France after his attack.

"Hajime," Raphael extended his hand as he welcomed his friend. "It's nice to see you again. How was the flight?"

Hajime shook the other man's hand and replied, "It's wonderful to be back. It was a good flight. We didn't have problems whatsoever. Thank you for asking." Hajime then turned towards Reina and reached for her. "Reina, this is Raphael, Alexandre's brother." Reina smiled and extended her hand to the man.

Hajime then went on to introduce Reina to one of his closest friends. "Raphael, this is Reina, my fiancée," he and Reina watched in amusement as the other man's eyes widened as he processed Reina's new title.

"Fiancée? That's wonderful news," Raphael pulled Reina to him and gave her a big hug. It stunned the young woman who didn't expect such an enthusiastic reaction from one of her intended's closest friends. A giggle erupted from her throat as she awkwardly returned his embrace and gave his back a soft pat.

As if realising he was being too forward, Raphael separated himself from Reina and holding her shoulders. "Pardon me, mademoiselle, I got too excited. I am just so happy for you and my friend here."

Reina found it adorable that the burly man in front of her blushed. Taking pity on his friend, Hajime clapped Raphael on the back before gently pulled Reina back to his side. It prompted Reina to comment, "It's fine, Raphael. I am so glad to finally meet you! Hajime told me so much about you."

Raphael's smile was gentle and sweet. He reached out to grab Reina's luggage and started leading the pair towards the exit. "It's wonderful to be meeting you to, Reina. Welcome to France."

A few hours after Raphael had left them to settle in at their hotel, Hajime was guiding Reina to where the Martinez' family restaurant. His good friend, Felipe's parents owned a Spanish restaurant.

Before leaving their room, Hajime had noticed that Reina was fidgety. She hadn't said anything but he knew that she was nervous meeting the important people in his life. She kept checking if the gifts they had brought back from Japan were okay and they didn't forget anything.

As they walked the streets, Hajime reached out and interlaced his fingers with Reina's free hand. She had to carry the gift bag but Hajime knew it was to keep her hand occupied to lessen her anxiety.

"Everything's going to be fine, love," Hajime reassured as they stopped at the stoplight, waiting to cross. "When Felipe's parents found out about me returning and also bringing you, they insisted in hosting a welcome dinner for the both of us. I know it's daunting to be subjected to a lot of people you don't know but they'll love you too. I'll be right there with you. Alexandre. Raphael. And of course, Felipe."

Reina forced herself to take a deep breath. "I'm being foolish, I know. It's just…these people are important to you."

The light turned green and they started walking again. Hajime gave her had a squeeze. "Yes, they are important to me but because they are important to me, they are equally aware how especially important you are to me. I love you. We are getting married. It's naturally they are excited to meet you and prepared this welcome party for the both of us."

"I believe you," the anxiety was pushed away for a moment before a thought crossed her mind and she asked, "Are you sure our gifts are okay? Should we have gotten wine or something else instead?"

Hajime couldn't help the laughter the bubbled up his throat. He quickly laid a kiss on the hand he was holding. "They'll appreciate the gifts we've brought. Besides, not to add to your anxiety but, they will actually be more interested in you."

"Yeah, that comment certainly didn't help at all," Reina replied dryly, causing another bout of laughter from Hajime. It wasn't long before she joined him in laughter.

The rest of the walk to the Martinez' was peaceful. Hajime would point now and then to share with Reina, "The boys and I would often have brunch at the cafe," "That's where I'd go whenever I got home sick," or, "That's where we sometime went to when we watched football matches." Reina was fascinated with everything Hajime was sharing with her. She loved learning about her fiancé's life when he lived in Paris. The commentaries also helped settle her nerves.

When they reached their destination, Hajime didn't have a chance to open the door to the restaurant. Felipe welcomed them with a huge grin. With open arms, both men gave each other man hug, giving each other some brisk slaps on each other's back.

"It's wonderful to have you back here with us, brother," Felipe said as he stood back. His gaze then fell to Reina, who felt her cheeks heat up at the sudden attention. "Welcome to France, Reina."

She gave him a smile as she stepped forward and offered her hand to shake, but Felipe was having none of that. He pulled the stunned woman to himself and hugged her before giving her the customary kiss on each cheek as a greeting. Reina's face blossomed into a redder hue. Without further ceremony, Felipe pulled Reina through the entrance with Hajime openly laughing as he followed. As soon as they all breached the thresh hold, a lot of hugs and kisses were exchanged as well as Reina's introduction to the fold.

It didn't take Hajime and Reina to realise that the party wasn't simply a welcome party but rather their engagement party. At one point, Raphael, Alexandre and Felipe were pulling Hajime away towards the other men at the other side of the room. Hajime hesitated since he did promise Reina he'd stay by her side to help settle her nerves.

Reina had heard the comment and excused herself from a conversation she was having with Felipe's older sister and turned to Hajime. She placed a hand and his chest before smiling and sharing a look at her intended's three closest, French friends. Hajime automatically placed his hand on top of hers.

"Go on be with the guys. It's been a while since you have been together. I'll be fine." With a gentle push, Reina encouraged Hajime, absolving him from his earlier promise.

His friends saw how Hajime's eyes had gentled as he looked at his beloved. They also noticed that Reina didn't bother changing the language to Japanese. Her encouragement for Hajime to go with the men was a complete opposite from when Hajime had been dating Juliette. During the short time Hajime was in a relationship with Juliette, the woman always tried to monopolise Hajime's time. She wanted to be the centre of Hajime's attention.

Reina gave Hajime another encouraging nod before to her previous conversation.

Hajime felt a hand settle on either of his shoulders.

"That's one special young lady," Alexandre commented before his brother, Raphael, added, "For a moment there, we were all worried about your tastes in women,"

Hajime snorted as the rest of the men started laughing. Walking towards the other side of the room, Hajime commented, "Before I forget, Reina and I have agreed to have our wedding in November.

Obviously, we don't have any formal invitations yet, but we both would like to extend an invitation to you. Hopefully it's enough time for you to arrange your schedules so you can join us in Japan."

CHAPTER 25

The tables had been arranged to form a long table. Food and drinks were abundant. Reina was delighted to see Spanish cuisine. There were several Spanish restaurants in Kyoto but Reina was excited to get to try it in Europe. Granted they were in Paris, from what she could tell, the Martinez family were proud of their heritage. Having grown up with a family that works hard to do their part in preserving traditional sweets, Reina could appreciate the tie between food and country. She was always ready to try something new outside her culture.

Hajime was amused watching Reina. For the past months, he and Reina had started of their own. It began then Hajime joined Reina when she would experiment with tea combination and desserts. The two expanded their exploration to all kinds of foods. Hajime had enjoyed introducing different kinds of cuisine and taste profiles to Reina.

"Try this, Rei. This is gambas al ajillo. I'm sure you'll like the combination of prawns, olive oil and garlic," Hajime offered.

Felipe, who decided to sit beside Reina, then held a plate of chicken croquettes towards the couple, "Here you go, you two. I've made these myself." Reina took the plate and set it between her and Hajime. Felipe turned to Reina and said, "These are some of Hajime's favourites."

After taking a bite and swallowing, "I can see why. Would you teach me how to make it?" Reina asked.

"Sure!" It wasn't a hard decision for Felipe. He was liking Hajime's fiancée more and more. He didn't miss the excitement on Reina's eyes when she saw the different food they were serving.

"Hajime mentioned you are a traditional sweets artisan but that wasn't your university course, right?" Felipe commented engaging Reina with a conversation.

"Yes. I finished with a degree in traditional Japanese literature and linguistics. But my family's shop has been the family legacy for over a hundred years." A whistle came out of Felipe's lips.

"Over a hundred years?" Felipe's sister, Ana exclaimed, joining into the conversation, "That's incredible!"

Reina smiled. "My family has been producing Japanese traditional sweets since the 1700s. But the shop was renamed to 'Amai Omoide' and relocated to Kyoto in 1860."

Jaws dropped around the table. Reina tilted her head to the side, wondering about the reactions she got. It was normal to have hundreds of years old, family businesses in Kyoto. There were even older ones near Amai Omoide. She knew one tea house, one she and her father often frequented when she was child, that was over 800 years old.

"That's a very rich and long family heritage," The Martinez patriarch, Emiliano, commented. "You are doing a wonderful thing in continuing that legacy, young lady."

Out of habit, Reina bowed in thanks to the Martinez patriarch. "Thank you, sir. It is an honour and a responsibility to protect it. My uncle has taken the responsibility of making sure it survives for future generations. Soon enough, it will fall on me."

"So, you are the heir?" Alexandre clarified.

Reina looked his direction and nodded. "I am the only heir for my generation."

Felipe decided to tease his friend. He looked at Hajime, a mischievous look on his face, "You have a responsibility to reproduce a lot of heirs then, my friend."

Reina automatically pinkened as Hajime cleared his throat and commented, "Any child will be welcomed when they come."

Looking back to Reina, Felipe commented, "My sisters, brother and I started helping in the kitchen here when we were kids. But I'm the only one who truly entered the culinary world."

"When I was born, dad was the one who took care of me since he worked with my uncle and grandparents at Amai Omoide. The store was originally the family house as well before a few generations ago, the family needed more living space. Until before we renovated, there was a small room at the side of the kitchen - a bedroom. It was where generations of Maruyamas were born and grew up in. My dad would leave me there. I almost quite literally grew up in that store. I also grew up watching and eventually learning how to create the sweets our store is known for."

"The boxes of sweets you gave us earlier," Martina, the Martinez family matriarch, asked, "Is that from your store?"

"No, Ma'am," Reina confirmed. She shared a quick look with Hajime and added, "They are best fresh so we finished making them at home before we left for the airport. But those are the same ones we do make for the store. And some are actually ideas we've been exploring – things we've been working on that are not for the store."

"We've been creating new recipes based on desserts and tea combinations we've tried." Hajime added.

"Are you planning to add the items to the store?" Felipe asked.

Hajime shook his head. "Amai Omoide is a traditional sweets shop. The ones we've been successful in creating so far are chocolate confections. Those we reserve for ourselves, family and friends. It's actually a product of a tradition we are building on. It started as a father-daughter thing with Rei and her dad. Now, we are hoping eventually pass on to our future kids."

Everybody could see how the couple's eyes soften as they shared eye contact and a smile.

Reina then said, "Will you tell me more about Spain, please? And the food? You have a wonderful restaurant here. I'm really fascinated about family-owned stores and their history."

The elder Martinez gave an indulgent smile and spent the next half-hour explaining how they decided to move to Paris and set up shop. They told Reina all about their hometown and what it was like living in Spain growing up. The younger members of the clan then shared some of their stories visiting relatives, spending summers with cousins and extended relatives, and how different the culture was from the French culture. Felipe and his siblings were all born in France. Reina was so engrossed with their stories that she missed Hajime's amused glance.

"You can't tell that she was so anxious before we came here. She was fussing about almost every little thing." Hajime commented as he, Raphael and Alexandre watched the rest of the party share stories.

"She pretty much sealed her honorary membership to the Martinez clan. They welcomed her because of you but based on her behaviour tonight – not to mention her fascination to the Martinez family history and native culture – she has been officially adopted into the fold." Raphael observed as the three men shared a laugh.

"Is it true her family's store has that long history? Not that I doubt what she says but it's a bit unimaginable for me." Alexandre said.

Hajime nodded. "Amai Omoide is over a century old but the Maruyama family has been wagashi artisans for longer. Her family's shop and my family's shrine are one of the oldest in our neighbourhood but certainly not the oldest in Kyoto. There are other old stores in our neighbourhood alone but Amai Omoide is definitely older than them by a few decades."

"And she's the only heir," Alexandre went on to comment.

"Yes, she is. It's the reason why I'm marrying into her family. Meaning, I will be the one to be added to their family register and change my name to continue on the Maruyama line."

The twins stopped, stunned for a moment. They processed the information they'd been given.

Hajime noticed his friends' reactions. He decided elucidate them more. "According to our laws dating back to the 19th century, married couples must choose either the husband's or the wife's name for official recording in the family registers. Granted, it is more common - even now - for women to be registered from her birth family's family register to her husband's. Around 5% are cases like mine. Inheritance and the importance of continuing the family line accounts for most, but not all. In some families, if there are no heirs, male or female, the head of the family adopts. After her uncle and father's generation, no male heir was born into the Maruyama clan to carry on the name. Reina must do it and I don't mind."

"But her uncle can still produce heirs, right?" Raphael inquired.

Hajime nodded. "Yes, he still can but it won't change Reina's status. She has already been named heir and has been groomed to take over the business and the family when the time came. When her uncle took over as the Maruyama family patriarch and head artisan, documents had been updated and with Rei's knowledge and blessing, he officially adopted her as his daughter. No names and titles changed. She still calls him uncle but legally, he is her father. There are legal documents declaring her as his legitimate heir regardless if he decides to have other children in the future – male or female. Ichigo, her uncle, told me it was to ensure that no matter what happened to him, Rei would not have to worry about anything. Her rights are protected, more than succession, just as he promised her father before he passed away."

"I can't imagine the pressure of carrying the legacy she is shouldering," Alexandre commented. He tried to put himself in Reina's situation. Perhaps being a twin will make it easier if it were him and Raphael but he knew it would have still been a heavy responsibility to bear. Looking at the younger woman, she didn't look at all bothered. Based on her answers earlier, she considered it an honour to take the responsibility on. "We just need to wrap up the embezzlement case you are involved in so that you both only need to worry about the future," he added.

Hajime gave a nod.

CHAPTER 26

Martina had offered to let Reina stay with her while Hajime was in court with Alexandre. Reina had thanked Felipe's mother but politely refused, saying she wanted to be there to support her fiancé. Alexandre had warned her that Juliette was more than likely going to be there. Felipe had then added that Juliette will try to flirt with Hajime.

Reina thanked them profusely for their warnings and concern but she was resolute in her decision. She had laid her hand on Hajime's arm, whom was standing next to her, and said, "We promised each other to face everything, good or bad, together. He stood beside me through my most challenging moments. I am not going to abandon him on his."

Felipe put his arm around Reina's shoulder and said, "Reina, since you're determined to go, I'm going to share some stories that will help put Juliette in her place. She can get really...challenging to deal with. But with the right comments here and there, it might be enough to silence her."

"Stop corrupting my fiancée, Felipe," Hajime laughed good-naturedly.

Felipe started laughing too but before he could say anything, Reina said, "It's not really corrupting, Hajime, if it's just an exchange of information." The men looked at her and saw the teasing glint in her eyes. "It's how you use the information," the playful smirk was enough to get all of them laughing.

Felipe held up a fist to Reina, which she bumped hers with. "You and I are going to get along just fine, princess."

"Princess?" Reina tilted her head, confused. She didn't expect Felipe to give her a nickname.

"'Reina' in Spanish means queen. Hajime will probably have my head if I refer to you as queen so you'll have to settle for princess, princess," Felipe explained. "But going about Juliette, just ignore her. You have, my brother, Hajime, here so that's all the defence you're going to need. As for offense,"

Reina patted Felipe hand. "I was brought up knowing how to deal with all kinds of people. Not to worry. I know how to deal with …difficult people too."

"Oh! Can I come with you guys then? I'd love to see Juliette's reaction. She definitely never expected you, princess," Felipe commented.

Hajime sighed and pulled Reina over to him. "All right, that's enough for one night. I have faith in Reina being able to stand her ground against Juliette. I'll be there if it gets out of hand."

***

The next day, Hajime and Reina met Alexandre at the lobby of their hotel. The men showed Reina where to get the best croissants for breakfast are. It was an enjoyable breakfast. Reina was regaled with countless stories of when Hajime and Alexandre were students and enjoyed breakfast at that cafe.

Hajime excused himself to go to the washroom. Alexandre put his coffee down. It was the first time he found himself alone with his friend's intended.

"I want to thank you for what you have done for my friend," Alexandre started. He saw the confusion that crossed Reina's eyes. He smiled before continuing, "When he left France, he was at the lowest part of his life. He had a lot of anger in him."

Reina's eyes cleared, showing she understood what he was saying. "Yes, he was at his lowest...especially about his attack."

"He told you about that," it was an observation on Alexandre's part.

Reina nodded. "I have to be honest though," she started. "It wasn't me, truly. He sought professional help on his own. I'm proud of him for it."

"Perhaps, but the fact that he opened his heart again and for it to soon blossom into marriage, I am relieved and extremely happy that he has made such progress."

The two shared a smile and enjoyed the comfortable silence that settled around them. A moment later, Reina decided to break it, "Can I ask you something?"

"Of course,"

Reina hesitated before continuing, "I really don't understand. Hajime told me that Pierre is Emily's only heir. Why embezzle from the business if you are you are going to inherit all of it anyway?"

Alexandre found another reason to appreciate his friend's intended. She had a reasonable and sharp mind. "It's actually a very good question. It came to light that Juliette was having an affair with Pierre while she was still in a relationship with Hajime. Before Hajime broke up with her, he had already been telling Felipe, Raphael and I about his suspicions. When he had reached his limit, Hajime broke it off. Unfortunately, it didn't look like an amicable split. Juliette is spiteful by nature so when Hajime broke up with her, she didn't like it. I believe she's the type of person who leaves people no longer useful to her, not the other way around. With Pierre taking over management because her aunt, Emily, became ill, Juliette manipulated him to satisfy her vindictive side."

"But she has been cleared from involvement by the police, right?" Reina asked, trying to follow the story.

Alexandre nodded. "There's not enough evidence. As an accountant, Juliette certainly has enough knowledge on how to manipulate the books. But again, there's no concrete evidence. No one can be charged with a crime without concrete evidence even if the suspicion is highly plausible."

Reina understood. Hajime had been accused and arrested under false evidence. No one deserved to be subjected to legal repercussions for faulty evidence. Satisfied with Alexandre's explanation, she went on to ask, "Is there anything I can do to make sure that Juliette doesn't make Hajime's life miserable? Do I need to do anything to stop whatever nonsense she plans on involving Hajime with?"

"Juliette is going to make you feel inferior and try to manipulate Hajime's emotions. She's the type of person who becomes ruthless to get what she wants. From what I've seen, what you and Hajime share is very strong. The only thing you need to do is to be yourself," Alexandre explained.

Reina nodded in acknowledgement. Alexandre's advice rang loudly in her brain a few hours later when Reina saw herself seated in the courtroom beside Hajime. Both of them were seated right behind Alexandre. She felt the cold glare directed towards her from the other side of the aisle. Hajime determinedly ignored Juliette just like she was. Reina and Hajime's hands were intertwined, with his thumb running back and forth on her knuckles.

It went on for the rest of the hearing. Reina took a short glance and was able to see how Juliette and Pierre looked. Juliette was indeed very beautiful with auburn hair that was styled to perfection. Her piercing green eyes would have been wonderful if they were only warm. There was an air around her that spoke of confidence. Pierre was clean cut with sharp features. He gave an impression of haughtiness.

Alexandre's explanation before the court session was running through Reina's mind. The police investigated all pertinent records and saw no concrete evidence to try Juliette in court. The criminal case against her had been dropped because of it. As for the defamation with illegal termination of Hajime against Pierre, the man had settled outside of court and a settlement had been awarded.

Alexandre had processed everything. Hajime's involvement with the legal cases he found himself in was about to end.

That day was the only day Hajime was required in court. He had to testify under oath and be cross-examined by Pierre's lawyer regarding the embezzlement issue. The entire time Hajime was on the stand, Reina kept her eyes on him. She was extremely proud of him. Hajime, for his part, never looked at the defence section of the courtroom. He completely ignored Pierre and Juliette. At times, his gaze would meet Reina, whom would offer him a small smile as a form of support.

The moment Hajime was excused from court, a feeling of closure washed over him. There wasn't more he needed to do in France. The only ties Hajime had left in Paris were his friends. He had waited for that day for a long time.

Hajime walked back to where Reina was seated. She smiled up and whispered as soon as he sat, "You did a great job, Hajime," he leaned closer to her and whispered back, "Thank you, love."

When court was adjourned, Alexandre walked with Hajime and Reina out of the courtroom. Outside, Juliette approached the group.

"Hajime," she said as she tried to put a hand of his person.

Hajime intercepted the hand by grabbing her wrist and pushed it away as he took a step back. He didn't say anything.

Juliette didn't seem to mind. She didn't even spare Reina a look. Juliette was determined to used her feminine wiles to seduce Hajime.

"I missed you," Juliette said.

Hajime lifted an eyebrow. His face remained cold. "Funny. I never thought about you at all," came his emotionless reply.

It was only then that Juliette deemed it necessary to glace at the young woman standing beside Hajime. Her features are Asian. Juliette looked down on Reina. With a sneer, Juliette tried to make Reina feel degraded, "You mean this girl has taken your attention? You'll grow tired of her soon," Juliette had spoken in rapid French, thinking that she wasn't understood by the other woman.

Reina raised an eyebrow of her own. "Are you much of a coward that you'd try to talk to someone, try to insult her in a language that you think she doesn't know?" Reina's voice was soft yet filled with steel. She replied in fluent French. "Perhaps you have to make sure the person you're trying to insult doesn't know the language you are using. It might actually work if that's the case."

Alexandre and Hajime had to stop themselves from laughing at the look of incredulity on Juliette's face.

Reina took a step closer to Juliette. She was going to do this and stand firm for Hajime and their future. "As for comment of growing tired of me, it would behove you to not assign your characteristics or misconstrued thoughts to Hajime. He's too much of a gentleman to lift a hand against you but I don't share the same restrictions. As a woman, I am within my rights to protect the people I love, especially my husband-to-be. So, if you have nothing nice to say, I'm sure I'm saying this in behalf of everyone here, it would do you well to walk away."

Having been taken completely by surprised, Juliette didn't know what to do. She usually had the control of any situation. She certainly didn't expect the young woman with Hajime to speak with her the way she did, not understand French.

Hajime wrapped an arm around Reina's waist and said, "You've heard my fiancée. Walk away. No one here is interested in anything you'd like to say."

With that, Hajime started to gently lead Reina forward. Alexandre followed without a word. As the three continued to walk out of the building, Reina commented, "Was that enough, Alexandre? You did say to be myself."

For a moment, Alexandre was stunned. He started laughing. "That was more than enough, princess."

Hajime tightened his arm around her waist and added, "That was awesome, love."

Reina released a relieved sigh. She just wanted Juliette out of their lives. Juliette had done enough to hurt Hajime in the past. In no way was Reina allowing the other woman another chance to inflict pain on Hajime. He was a grown man who could take care of himself but given his history with Juliette, Reina decided to take it upon herself to take care of Juliette herself.

"You were fierce, princess," Alexandre commented.

"I could never tolerate other people trying to bully or hurt people I love," Reina replied.

"That never changed from when you were a child. You'd always been a fierce protector," Hajime commented.

Reina commented, "What do you expect? Growing up with you and your brothers, plus Eito, certainly helped me develop that way."

Hajime removed his arm from Reina's waist and reached for her hand. "Anyway, that's that. Let's now concentrate on our future instead."

EPILOGUE

1869, Second year of Meiji

Riku and Shiori were relieved to be back home in Kyoto. It had been a few years since they left. Satsuma was peaceful, and Keisuke had kept his word. His clan had truly sheltered the Maruyama family. They were kind people. Keisuke also introduced Riku to his patient, the sweet potato farmer. Riku loved satsuma-imo as soon as he tried it, so he and the boys would help the farmer, learning what they could about growing, taking care of the sweet potatoes, the best time to harvest, and how to cook them properly. All the while, Shiori helped Keisuke at his clinic. Keisuke also took the time to make sure that Shiori's pregnancy progressed well.

They were all surprised when she gave birth to twin girls, Kanami and Erika. They had expected Kanami. Erika, the younger of the twins, was the surprise. There was a moment when Keisuke thought he might lose both mother and baby because of some complications. Shiori had started bleeding excessively and the second baby took her time coming. But Shiori was a fighter and so was her daughter. After a tense hour, the second baby finally came out, all pink and crying with a full set of lungs. It was how she got her name, blessed.

Life in Kagoshima was near perfect for the Maruyamas, but they knew that Kyoto was home. With Keisuke's close counsel, they kept an ear out for what was happening at the capital. They had learned about the Satsuma and Choshu alliance – the Satcho alliance.

Keisuke had explained that while the two were traditionally fierce enemies, with the Satsuma taking a moderate stance in maintaining the status quo and the Choshu were aggressive in trying to overthrow the government, Satsuma and Choshu agreed to an alliance. Satsuma leaders, Saigo Takamori and Okubo Toshimichi, were brought together with the Choshu leader, Katsura Kogoro. Sakamoto Ryoma, from the Tosa domain, mediated between the two domains. All leaders agreed that it was time for change and agreed to assist one another in the chance that one of their domains were attacked.

With the Choshu desperately needing modern weaponry that the Satsuma had access to due to their considerable arms trade with Great Britain, Sakamoto used the knowledge of Choshu to suggest a weapon supply agreement for the fight against the Tokugawa shogunate. Saigo brokered the agreement. But regardless of the agreement, there was still a high level of distrust between the two domains.

But when the Shogunate demanded the retirement and confinement of the Choshu leader, Mori Takachika, and the reduction of the domain revenues, it enraged the Choshu leadership which led the formal, six-point agreement with Satsuma.

It was a limited agreement with the Satsuma initially agreed to obtain a pardon for Choshu from the imperial court. It was understood that if the imperial pardon wasn't obtained and the Shogunate attacked, Satsuma would engage by sending over 2000 troops to Kyoto with a caveat that Satsuma would only do so if the Kuwana and Aizu domains, or Yoshinobu Tokugawa's personal guard attempted to block Satsuma's access to the emperor.

The Alliance proved to be crucial for the Choshu domain in overcoming the punitive expedition – known as the second Choshu expedition - mounted against them by the Tokugawa shogunate in the summer of 1866.

The couple further learned about the Satcho Alliance's role at the Battle of Toba-Fushimi in Kyoto. Pro-Imperial forces, led by the Satsuma, Choshu, and Tosa domains, fought the Tokugawa shogunate at

Fushimi, Kyoto. The battle lasted only four days but the outcome started the end of the centuries of Tokugawa shogunate.

The bloody encounter made the couple glad they accepted Keisuke's invitation to Kagoshima.

They all watched from within the safety of the Satsuma domain as the centuries-old Tokugawa regime fell, making way for the Meiji era. Since the Boshin war – also known as the Japanese Revolution or Civil War, started with shots fired at Koeda Bridge, Toba, Kyoto and Fushimi road, Kyoto - waged until the summer of 1869, Riku remained cautious and decided to stay at Kagoshima. When word of the war's end reached them, they headed home in autumn of 1869. The community they became a part of saw them off, and promises of future visits were exchanged.

Riku had established a partnership for supplies of sweet potatoes, which he'd be using in some of the wagashi served at Amai Omoide.

Being at Satsuma and cultivating relationships with different people made Riku appreciate life more. It had been hard to keep moving, fearing violence, fearing death, but they had grown stronger in their struggled to survive. They helped when they could. They respected people regardless of their social standing.

And finally, they were home. It was the start of another chapter for Riku, his family, and for Amai Omoide.

NAME PRONUNCIATION GUIDE

DESCRIPTION	MEANINGS OF THE NAME	
Main Character	**MARUYAMA (丸山)**	**REINA (怜成)**
	Round Mountain	Clever, wise To become, to accomplish
Main Character	**YOSHIDA (吉田)**	**HAJIME (原)**
	Lucky (or good) Rice paddy	Origin, source, foundation
Maruyama Reina's Uncle	**MARUYAMA (丸山)**	**ICHIGO (一護)**
	Round Mountain	One Protection, safeguard, defend
Maruyama Reina's Father	**MARUYAMA (丸山)**	**YUUKI (祐喜)**
	Round Mountain	Help, assist, protect Joy, rejoice, pleasure

Maruyama Reina's Mother	**SUZUKI (鈴木)**	**REIKA (冷夏)**
	Ears of the rice piled up	Cool, cold, chilled Summer, hot, warmth
Maruyama Reina's Stepfather	**SUZUKI (鈴木)**	**YUITO (結斗)**
	Ears of the rice piled up	Bind, to finish, end Suddenly, abruptly
Maruyama Reina's Grandmother	**MARUYAMA (丸山)**	**YUZUKI (雪月花)**
	Round Mountain	Snow Moon Flower
Maruyama Reina's Grandfather	**MARUYAMA (丸山)**	**KOUJI (交二)**
	Round Mountain	Exchange, mix Two
Yoshida Hajime's Father	**YOSHIDA (吉田)**	**ISSEI (一清)**
	Lucky (or good) Rice paddy	One Pure, clear, clean

Yoshida Hajime's Mother	**YOSHIDA (吉田)**	**YUUKA (優花)**
	Lucky (or good) Rice paddy	Gentleness, kindness Flower
Yoshidas' Oldest Son	**YOSHIDA (吉田)**	**ITSUKI (一毅)**
	Lucky (or good) Rice paddy	One Perseverance, fortitude, determination
Yoshidas' Second Son	**YOSHIDA (吉田)**	**MASASHI (真士)**
	Lucky (or good) Rice paddy	Truth, reality, genuine Samurai, warrior, gentleman
Yoshida Itsuki's Wife	**YOSHIDA (吉田)**	**HARUKA (永)**
	Lucky (or good) Rice paddy	Eternity, permanence
Yoshidas' Youngest Son	**YOSHIDA (吉田)**	**TATSUNORI (達則)**
	Lucky (or good) Rice paddy	Reach, arrive, attain, achieve Rule, regulation, principle

Amai Omoide Staff	**ITO (伊藤)**	**SAYAKA (快)**
	Clothing Wisteria	Pleasant, comfortable, agreeable
Amai Omoide Staff	**FUJIWARA (藤原)**	**MIO (美夜)**
	Wisteria field	Brevity, beauty, pretty Night, evening
Yoshida Hajime's Best Friend	**YAMANE (山根)**	**EITO (瑛士)**
	Mountain root	Brightness, clarity, sparkle Samurai, warrior, gentleman
Maruyama Reina's upperclassman	**FUJII (藤井)**	**SATOSHI (智)**
	Well of Wisteria	Wisdom, intellect, knowledge
Maruyama Reina's Best Friend	**HARADA (原田)**	**AIKA (和佳)**
	Rice paddy on the plain	Harmony, peace, concord Excellent, beautiful, good